D0579640

THE USBORNE PICTURE DICTIONARY IN FRENCH

Felicity Brooks and Mairi Mackinnon

Designer and modelmaker: Jo Litchfield

French language consultant: Lorraine Beurton-Sharp

Design and additional illustrations by
Mike Olley and Brian Voakes

Photography by Howard Allman

Contents

How to say the words

You can hear all the French words in this book, read by a French person, on the Usborne Quicklinks Web site at **www.usborne-quicklinks.com**
All you need is an Internet connection and a computer that can play sounds. Find out more on page 112.

Using your dictionary

You can use this dictionary to find out how to say things in French. Every page has 12 main words in English, with the same words in French (the translations).

The English words are in the order of the alphabet: words beginning with A are first in the book. There are also pictures to show what words mean.

This letter in a blue square shows the first letter of the English words on that page.

This word shows the first English word on the page.

This word shows the last English word on the page.

All the English words are shown in blue. The French translations are shown in black.

Don't forget that in a dictionary you read down the page in columns. In most other books you read across.

Short sentences or phrases, in English and in French, show you how the word can be used.

If you forget the order of the letters in the alphabet, look at the bottom of any page.

S start *to* stool

start   commencer
The birds are starting to eat the seeds.
Les oiseaux commencent à manger les graines.

station   la gare
There are two trains in the station.
Il y a deux trains dans la gare.

stay   rester,
(visit) loger
The cows stay in the field.
Les vaches restent dans le champ.
I'm staying with my aunt.
Je loge chez ma tante.

steep   raide
It's a steep path.
C'est un sentier raide.

stick¹   le bâton
(twig) la brindille
a stick for my dog
un bâton pour mon chien

stick²   coller
Polly is sticking her drawing to the wall.
Polly colle son dessin au mur.

still¹   (calm) tranquille,
(not moving) immobile
Milo is staying still.
Milo reste tranquille.
The car is standing still.
La voiture est immobile.

still²   encore
Oliver's still hungry.
Oliver a encore faim.
He still has some apples.
Il a encore des pommes.

sting   piquer
Amy is afraid that the bee will sting her.
Amy a peur que l'abeille la pique.

stir   remuer
Jack is stirring the mixture.
Jack remue le mélange.

stone   la pierre
stones from the garden.
des pierres du jardin

stool   le tabouret
a small, blue stool
un petit tabouret bleu

a b c d e f g h i j k l m n o p q r s t u v w x y z

Sometimes the same English word appears twice with little numbers next to it. This shows that the same word can be used in two different ways. The French translations may look very different.

The blue letter also shows the first letter of the English words on that page.

How to find a word

1 Think of the letter the word starts with. "Stone" starts with an "s", for example.

2 Look through the dictionary until you have found the "s" pages.

3 Think of the next letter of the word. Look for words that begin with "st".

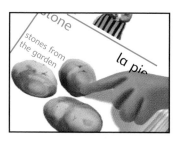

4 Now look down all the "st" words until you find your word.

Le or la?

In French, all nouns, or "naming" words such as "boy" and "house", are either masculine or feminine. The French word for "the" is *le* for masculine nouns, and *la* for feminine nouns.

Sometimes you can guess whether a noun is masculine or feminine – for example, "boy" is masculine (*le garçon*). Other times, you need to check in the dictionary.

If a noun begins with *a, e, i, o,* or *u,* and sometimes *h,* then *le* or *la* is shortened to *l'.* The letter *(m)* or *(f)* after the noun tells you whether it is masculine or feminine.

Masculine or feminine?

Which of these fruits are masculine, and which are feminine?

la fraise

le citron

la cerise

la framboise

le raisin

l'ananas (m)

la pomme

la banane

Answers: ananas, citron and raisin are masculine. Banane, cerise, fraise, framboise and pomme are feminine.

Looking at a word

When you look up a word, here are some of the things you can find out.

These words in brackets show that you can use the word in different ways.

You can check how to spell the word in English.

know (people) (facts) connaître, savoir

If the word can be used in different ways, there may be more than one French translation.

Sam knows these children.
Sam connaît ces enfants.

You can see how you might use the word in English and in French.

I know he is angry.
Je sais qu'il est fâché.

If the word can be used in different ways, there are different phrases or sentences.

You can see a picture of the word, or a way of using the word.

Plurals

"Plural" means "more than one". The French for "the" when you are talking about more than one is *les*, for both masculine and feminine nouns. You also add *s* to the end of the noun, as you do in English:

boy   le garçon
boys   les garçons

If the noun ends in *s* already, you don't need to add another *s*:

mice   les souris

For a very few nouns, you add *x* or other letters instead of *s*. In this dictionary, these plurals are shown like this:

knee   le genou (genoux)

Adjectives

"Describing" words, such as "small" or "expensive", are called adjectives. In French, they usually go after the noun they are describing. The endings change, depending whether the noun is masculine or feminine, singular or plural. For example, the French for "hot" is *chaud*:

hot bath   le bain chaud

For a feminine noun, you add *e* to the end of the adjective (unless it ends in *e* already):

hot water l'eau chaude

For masculine plurals, you add *s* to the end of the adjective (unless it ends in *s* or *x* already):

hot dishes les plats chauds

For feminine plurals, you add *es*:

hot drinks les boissons chaudes

A few adjectives have slightly different feminine forms. They are shown in the dictionary like this:

soft doux (douce)

A very few also have a different form before masculine nouns beginning with *a, e, i, o, u,* and sometimes *h*. They are shown like this:

old vieux (vieil, vieille)

Find out more about using adjectives on page 97 at the back of the book.

Verbs

"Doing" words, such as "walk" or "laugh", are called verbs. In English, verbs don't change very much, whoever is doing them:

I walk, you walk, he walks

In French, the endings change much more. Many verbs work in a similar way to the one below. The verb is in the present – the form that you use to talk about what is happening now.

to give	donner
I give	je donne
you give*	tu donnes
he gives	il donne
she gives	elle donne
we give	nous donnons
you give*	vous donnez
they give	ils donnent
	elles donnent

In the main part of the dictionary, when you look up a verb you will find the "to" form, together with a sentence or phrase to show how the verb can be used. Most of these sentences use the verb in the present.

On pages 101-104 at the back of the book, you will find a list of all the verbs, with the most useful forms in the present: the "to" form, the "he" or "she" form, and the "I" form and "they" form if they are very different.

Two useful verbs

Two of the most useful verbs to know are "to be" and "to have". Here they are in French, in the present form:

to be	être
I am	je suis
you are*	tu es
he is	il est
she is	elle est
we are	nous sommes
you are*	vous êtes
they are	ils sont, elles sont

to have	avoir
I have	j'ai
you have*	tu as
he has	il a
she has	elle a
we have	nous avons
you have*	vous avez
they have	ils ont, elles ont

Mostly, you use them in just the same way as you do in English:

He is happy Il est content

She is angry Elle est fâchée

I have an apple
        J'ai une pomme

They have a cold
        Ils ont une rhume

Just sometimes, it isn't the verb you expect:

to be afraid	avoir peur
to be cold	avoir froid
to be hot	avoir chaud
to be hungry	avoir faim
to be thirsty	avoir soif

* In French, you use "tu" for one person, either a young person or someone you know very well. You use "vous" for more than one person, or for an older person or someone you don't know very well.

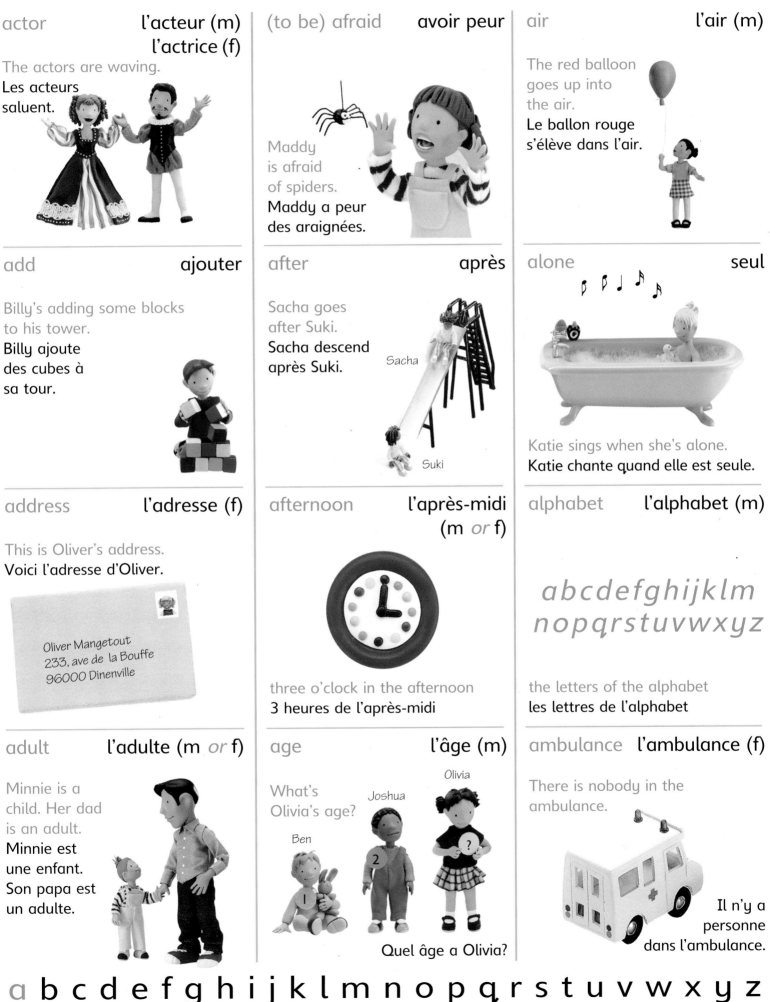

actor　l'acteur (m)
　　　　　l'actrice (f)

The actors are waving.
Les acteurs saluent.

(to be) afraid　avoir peur

Maddy is afraid of spiders.
Maddy a peur des araignées.

air　l'air (m)

The red balloon goes up into the air.
Le ballon rouge s'élève dans l'air.

add　ajouter

Billy's adding some blocks to his tower.
Billy ajoute des cubes à sa tour.

after　après

Sacha goes after Suki.
Sacha descend après Suki.

Sacha

Suki

alone　seul

Katie sings when she's alone.
Katie chante quand elle est seule.

address　l'adresse (f)

This is Oliver's address.
Voici l'adresse d'Oliver.

Oliver Mangetout
233, ave de la Bouffe
96000 Dinenville

afternoon　l'après-midi (m *or* f)

three o'clock in the afternoon
3 heures de l'après-midi

alphabet　l'alphabet (m)

abcdefghijklm nopqrstuvwxyz

the letters of the alphabet
les lettres de l'alphabet

adult　l'adulte (m *or* f)

Minnie is a child. Her dad is an adult.
Minnie est une enfant. Son papa est un adulte.

age　l'âge (m)

What's Olivia's age?

Ben

Joshua

Olivia

Quel âge a Olivia?

ambulance　l'ambulance (f)

There is nobody in the ambulance.

Il n'y a personne dans l'ambulance.

a b c d e f g h i j k l m n o p q r s t u v w x y z

amount　　la quantité

a large amount
of pasta
une grande
quantité de
pâtes

ankle　　la cheville

Ankles join legs
to feet.

Les
chevilles
joignent
les jambes
aux pieds.

apple　　la pomme

It's good to eat apples.
Il est bon de
manger des
pommes.

angel　　l'ange (m)

a Christmas angel
un ange
de Noël

answer　　la réponse

Question: Which animal
says meow?
Answer: A cat.
Question: Quel
animal miaule?
Réponse: Le chat.

arm　　le bras

This is Jack's
left arm.
Voici le bras
gauche de
Jack.

angry　　fâché

Jack is angry with Pip.
Jack est fâché
avec Pip.

ant　　la fourmi

Ants like sugar.
Les fourmis aiment
le sucre.

arrive　　arriver

The bus arrives at one o'clock.
Le bus arrive à 1 heure.

animal　　l'animal (m)
(animaux)

A lion is an
animal.

Le lion est
un animal.

ape　　le singe

An orangutan
is a kind of
ape.

L'orang-
outan
est une
espèce
de singe.

art　　l'art (m)

It's a work of art.
C'est une
oeuvre
d'art.

a b c d e f g h i j k l m n o p q r s t u v w x y z

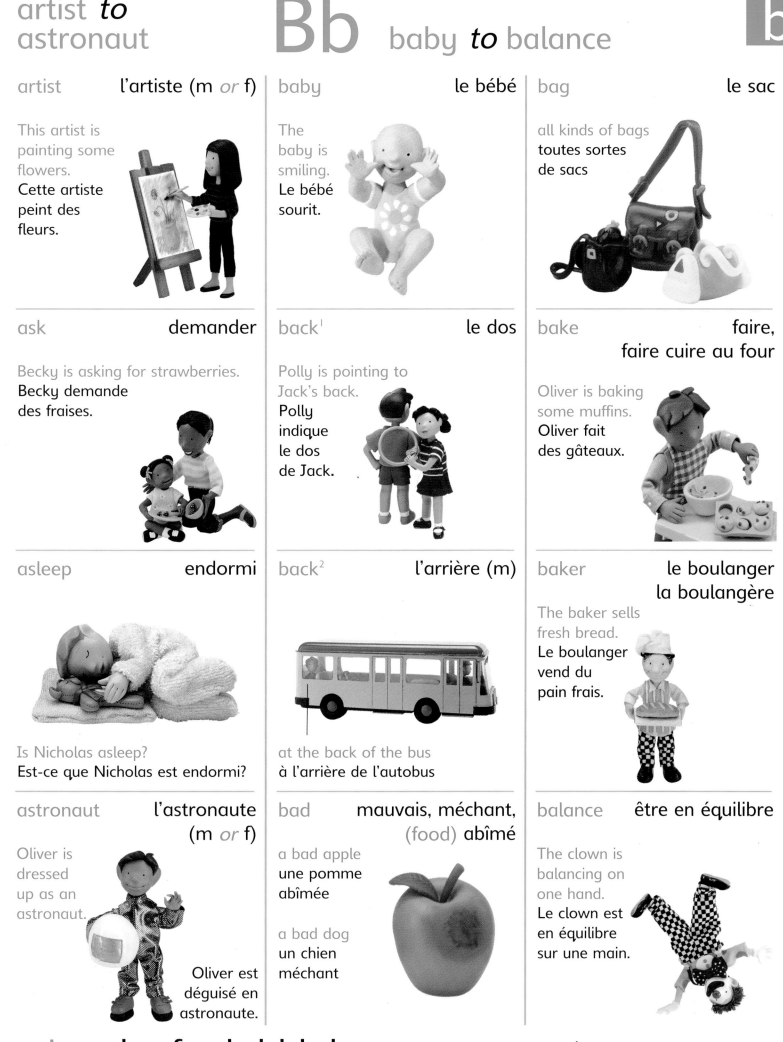

artist　l'artiste (m *or* f)

This artist is painting some flowers.
Cette artiste peint des fleurs.

ask　demander

Becky is asking for strawberries.
Becky demande des fraises.

asleep　endormi

Is Nicholas asleep?
Est-ce que Nicholas est endormi?

astronaut　l'astronaute (m *or* f)

Oliver is dressed up as an astronaut.
Oliver est déguisé en astronaute.

baby　le bébé

The baby is smiling.
Le bébé sourit.

back[1]　le dos

Polly is pointing to Jack's back.
Polly indique le dos de Jack.

back[2]　l'arrière (m)

at the back of the bus
à l'arrière de l'autobus

bad　mauvais, méchant, (food) abîmé

a bad apple
une pomme abîmée

a bad dog
un chien méchant

bag　le sac

all kinds of bags
toutes sortes de sacs

bake　faire, faire cuire au four

Oliver is baking some muffins.
Oliver fait des gâteaux.

baker　le boulanger la boulangère

The baker sells fresh bread.
Le boulanger vend du pain frais.

balance　être en équilibre

The clown is balancing on one hand.
Le clown est en équilibre sur une main.

a b **c** d e f g h i j k l m n o p q r s t u v w x y **z**

bald *to* bark

bald — **chauve**

Mr. Rogers is bald.
Monsieur Rogers est chauve.

banana — **la banane**

A banana is a yellow fruit.
La banane est un fruit jaune.

bar — **la barre**

a steel bar
une barre en acier

Hold onto the bar!
Tiens bien la barre!

ball — **le ballon**

a brightly colored ball
un ballon aux couleurs vives

band — **l'orchestre (m)**

Polly and Marco play in a band.
Polly et Marco jouent dans un orchestre.

bare — **nu**

Marcus is bare for his bath.
Marcus est nu pour aller dans son bain.

ballerina — **la ballerine**

Lucy is a ballerina.
Lucy est ballerine.

bang — **boum**

Bang! The balloon bursts.
Boum !!!
Boum! Le ballon éclate.

bark¹ — **l'écorce (f)**

the bark of a tree
l'écorce d'un arbre

balloon — **le ballon, (hot air) la montgolfière**

a pink balloon
un ballon rose

a balloon ride
un voyage en montgolfière

bank — **la banque**

Mr. Brand is getting money from the bank.
Monsieur Brand retire de l'argent à la banque.

bark² — **aboyer**

Pip is barking.
Pip aboie.

Wouah! Wouah!

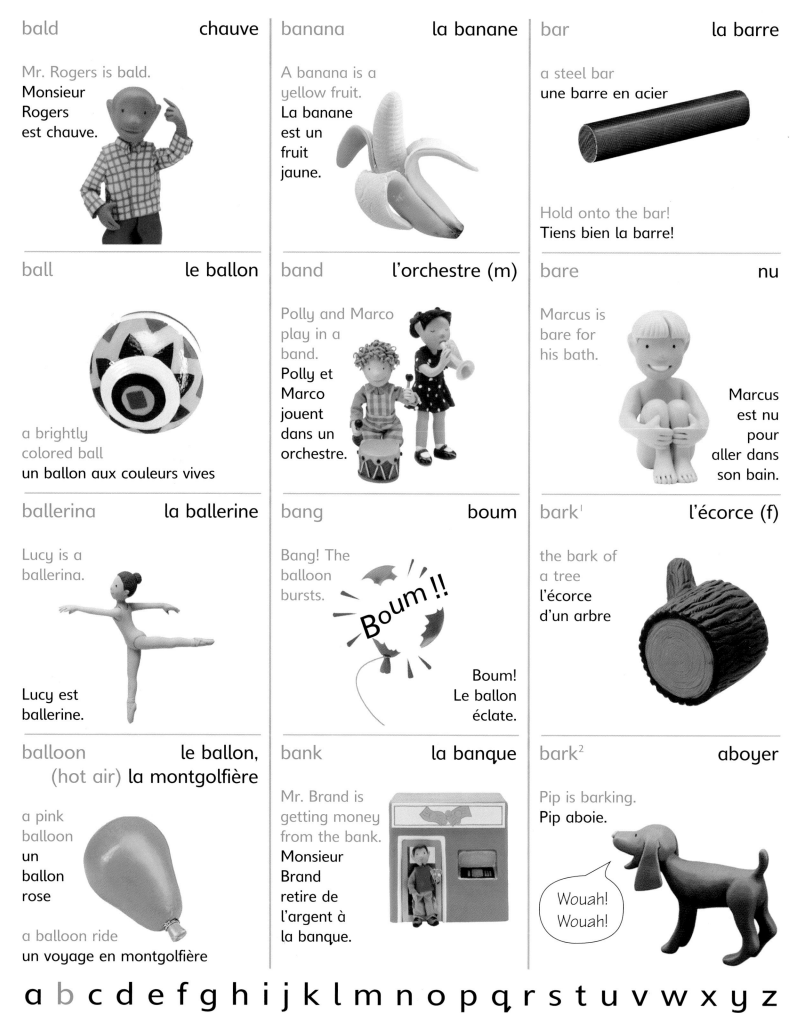

a b c d e f g h i j k l m n o p q r s t u v w x y z

barn *to* bed

barn   la grange

The barn is full of hay.
La grange est remplie de foin.

bathtub   la baignoire

The bathtub is empty.
La baignoire est vide.

bear   l'ours (m)

A bear is a wild animal.
L'ours est un animal sauvage.

base   le pied

The lamp has a yellow base.
La lampe a un pied jaune.

beach   la plage

They are playing on the beach.
Ils jouent sur la plage.

beard   la barbe

Mr. Brown has a beard.
Monsieur Brown a une barbe.

basket   le panier

a big, round basket
un grand panier rond

beak   le bec

A toucan has a big beak.
Le toucan a un grand bec.

beautiful   beau (bel, belle)*

a beautiful pink cake
un beau gâteau rose

bat (animal) la chauve-souris, **(for sports)** la batte

A bat isn't a bird.
La chauve-souris n'est pas un oiseau.

a baseball bat
une batte de base-ball

bean   le haricot

green beans
les haricots verts

bed   le lit

a child's bed
un lit d'enfant

a b c d e f g h i j k l m n o p q r s t u v w x y z

* masculine plural form: *beaux*

9

bedroom   **la chambre**

Ben's bedroom   la chambre de Ben

before   **avant**

Suki goes before Sacha.
Suki descend avant Sacha.

Sacha

Suki

below   **sous**

The kitten is below the boards.

Le chaton est sous les planches.

bee   **l'abeille (f)**

Honey comes from bees.
Le miel provient des abeilles.

begin   **commencer**

Sam's beginning to fall asleep.
Sam commence à s'endormir.

belt   **la ceinture**

a brown leather belt
une ceinture marron en cuir

beetle   **le scarabée**

Beetles have six legs.
Les scarabées ont six pattes.

behind   **derrière**

The kitten is behind the flowerpot.
Le chaton est derrière le pot de fleurs.

beside   **à côté**

The kitten is beside the flowerpot.
Le chaton est à côté du pot de fleurs.

beetroot   **la betterave**

Beetroot grows underground.
La betterave pousse sous terre.

belong   **appartenir**

The book belongs to Suzie.
Le livre appartient à Suzie.

between   **entre**

The kitten is between the two flowerpots.

Le chaton est entre les deux pots de fleurs.

a b c d e f g h i j k l m n o p q r s t u v w x y z

10

bib — le bavoir

a baby's bib
un bavoir de bébé

birthday — l'anniversaire (m)

a birthday party
une fête d'anniversaire

boat — le bateau (bateaux)

a rowboat
un bateau à rames

bicycle — le vélo, la bicyclette

Sara's blue bicycle
le vélo bleu de Sara

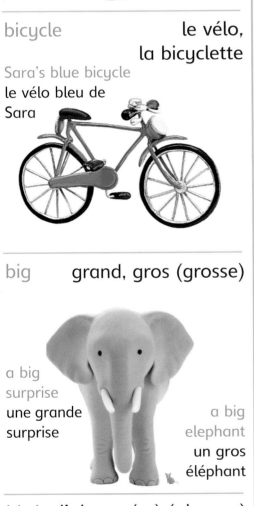

bite — mordre, (food) croquer

Jon is biting an apple.

Jon croque une pomme.

Our dog doesn't bite.

Notre chien ne mord pas.

body — le corps

some parts of the body
des parties du corps

arm
le bras

tummy
le ventre

leg
la jambe

foot
le pied

big — grand, gros (grosse)

a big surprise
une grande surprise

a big elephant
un gros éléphant

blanket — la couverture

a wool blanket
une couverture de laine

bone — l'os (m)

Patch has found some bones.
Patch a trouvé des os.

bird — l'oiseau (m) (oiseaux)

There are some birds that can't fly.

Il y a des oiseaux qui ne volent pas.

blow — souffler

Polly is blowing out the candles.
Polly souffle les bougies.

book — le livre

Tina is reading a book.
Tina lit un livre.

a b c d e f g h i j k l m n o p q r s t u v w x y z

boot   la botte

Alex puts on boots when it's raining.

Alex met des bottes quand il pleut.

bottle   la bouteille

plastic and glass bottles
des bouteilles en plastique et en verre

bottom¹   le derrière

Jack's bottom is in the circle.

Le derrière de Jack est dans le cercle.

bottom²   le bas

The kitten is at the bottom of the stairs.

Le chaton est en bas de l'escalier.

bowl   le bol

a plastic bowl
un bol en plastique

box   la boîte

a cardboard box
une boîte en carton

boy   le garçon

Oliver and Robert are boys.

Oliver et Robert sont des garçons.

branch   la branche

two birds on a branch

deux oiseaux sur une branche

brave   courageux (courageuse)

Mr. Sparks is very brave. Monsieur Sparks est très courageux.

bread   le pain

a loaf of bread
un pain

break   casser

Asha has broken the vase. Asha a cassé le vase.

breakfast   le petit déjeuner

a healthy breakfast
un petit déjeuner sain

a b c d e f g h i j k l m n o p q r s t u v w x y z

breathe — **respirer**

Divers breathe air from tanks.

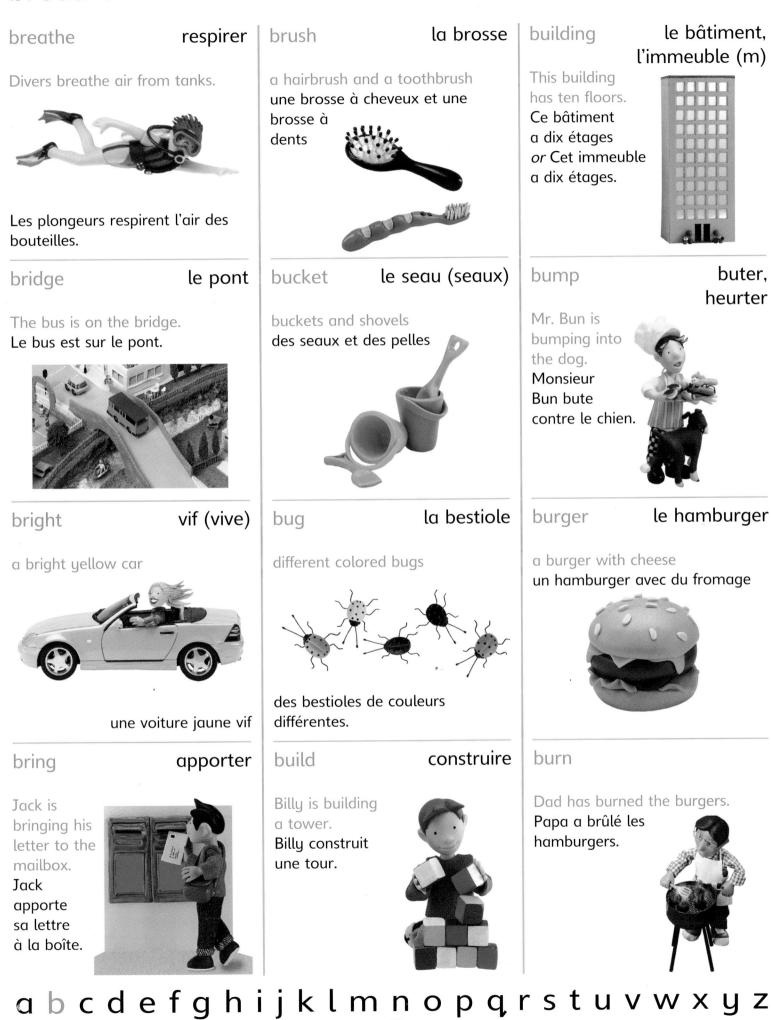

Les plongeurs respirent l'air des bouteilles.

bridge — **le pont**

The bus is on the bridge.
Le bus est sur le pont.

bright — **vif (vive)**

a bright yellow car

une voiture jaune vif

bring — **apporter**

Jack is bringing his letter to the mailbox.
Jack apporte sa lettre à la boîte.

brush — **la brosse**

a hairbrush and a toothbrush
une brosse à cheveux et une brosse à dents

bucket — **le seau (seaux)**

buckets and shovels
des seaux et des pelles

bug — **la bestiole**

different colored bugs

des bestioles de couleurs différentes.

build — **construire**

Billy is building a tower.
Billy construit une tour.

building — **le bâtiment, l'immeuble (m)**

This building has ten floors.
Ce bâtiment a dix étages *or* Cet immeuble a dix étages.

bump — **buter, heurter**

Mr. Bun is bumping into the dog.
Monsieur Bun bute contre le chien.

burger — **le hamburger**

a burger with cheese
un hamburger avec du fromage

burn

Dad has burned the burgers.
Papa a brûlé les hamburgers.

a b c d e f g h i j k l m n o p q r s t u v w x y z

bus   le bus

The bus is going into town.
Le bus va en ville.

bush   le buisson

Bushes are smaller than trees.
Les buissons sont plus petits que les arbres.

a bush
un buisson

a tree
un arbre

busy   occupé

Mr. Bun is busy in the kitchen.
Monsieur Bun est occupé à la cuisine.

butcher   le boucher
la bouchère

Mrs. Beef is a butcher.

Madame Beef est bouchère.

butter   le beurre

some butter for my sandwiches
du beurre pour mes sandwichs

butterfly   le papillon

Butterflies are insects.

Les papillons sont des insectes.

button   le bouton

four brightly colored buttons
quatre boutons aux couleurs vives

buy   acheter

Suzie is buying an apple.
Suzie achète une pomme.

café   le café

Suzie and her dad are having lunch at the café.
Suzie et son papa déjeunent au café.

Café Delargo

cage   la cage

a small cage   une petite cage

cake   le gâteau

a delicious cake
un gâteau délicieux

calf   le veau

a cow and her calf
une vache et son veau

a b c d e f g h i j k l m n o p q r s t u v w x y z

call — appeler

Alex is calling Pip.
Alex appelle Pip.

Viens, Pip!

camel — le chameau (chameaux)

A camel can have one or two humps.

Un chameau peut avoir une ou deux bosses.

camera — l'appareil photo (m)

This camera is easy to use.
Cet appareil photo est facile à utiliser.

camp — faire du camping

They are camping.
Ils font du camping.

candle — la bougie

a cake with eight candles
un gâteau avec huit bougies

cap — la casquette

a baseball cap
une casquette de base-ball

car — l'auto (f), la voiture

a sports car
une voiture de sport

card — la carte

I have three birthday cards.
J'ai trois cartes d'anniversaire.

carpet — la moquette

a room with blue carpet

une pièce avec de la moquette bleue

carrot — la carotte

Carrots are vegetables.

Les carottes sont des légumes.

carry — porter

Aggie is carrying some flowers.
Aggie porte des fleurs.

castle — le château (châteaux)

an old castle — un vieux château

a b c d e f g h i j k l m n o p q r s t u v w x y z

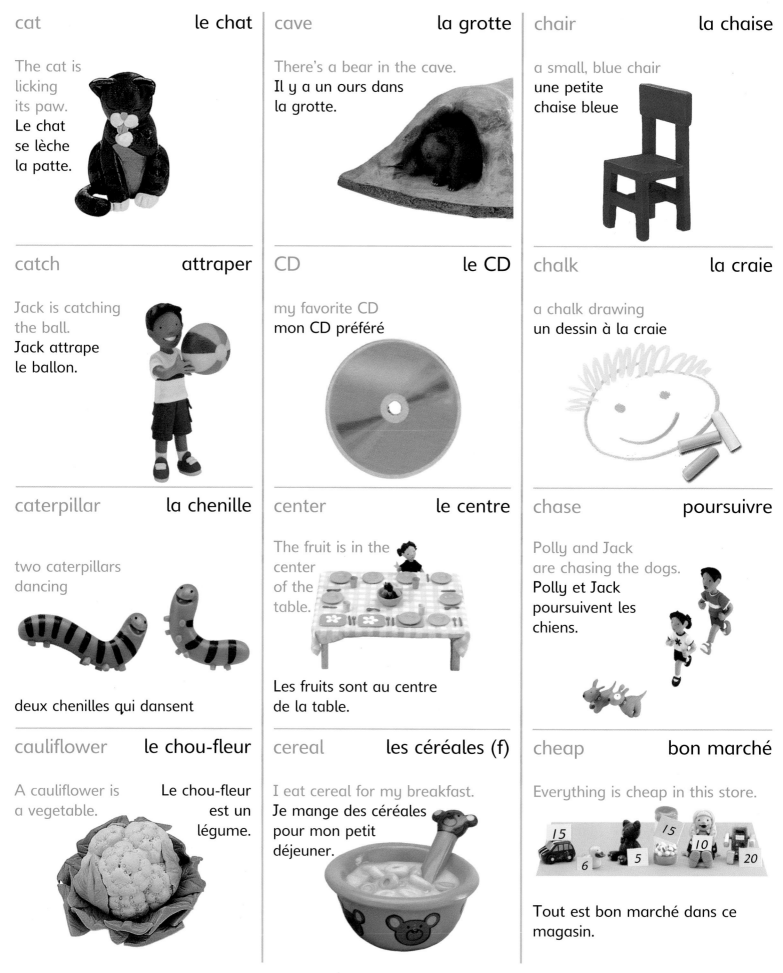

cat — le chat

The cat is licking its paw.
Le chat se lèche la patte.

cave — la grotte

There's a bear in the cave.
Il y a un ours dans la grotte.

chair — la chaise

a small, blue chair
une petite chaise bleue

catch — attraper

Jack is catching the ball.
Jack attrape le ballon.

CD — le CD

my favorite CD
mon CD préféré

chalk — la craie

a chalk drawing
un dessin à la craie

caterpillar — la chenille

two caterpillars dancing

deux chenilles qui dansent

center — le centre

The fruit is in the center of the table.

Les fruits sont au centre de la table.

chase — poursuivre

Polly and Jack are chasing the dogs.
Polly et Jack poursuivent les chiens.

cauliflower — le chou-fleur

A cauliflower is a vegetable.
Le chou-fleur est un légume.

cereal — les céréales (f)

I eat cereal for my breakfast.
Je mange des céréales pour mon petit déjeuner.

cheap — bon marché

Everything is cheap in this store.

Tout est bon marché dans ce magasin.

a b c d e f g h i j k l m n o p q r s t u v w x y z

cheese   le fromage

Swiss cheese
du fromage suisse

chicken   le poulet

I like roast chicken.
J'aime le poulet rôti.

choose   choisir

Billy is choosing between the apple and the cake.
Billy choisit entre la pomme et le gâteau.

chef   le chef cuisinier

Mr. Cook is a chef.
Monsieur Cook est chef cuisinier.

child   l'enfant (m *or* f)

three children   **trois enfants**

city   la grande ville

There are a lot of buildings in a city.
Il y a beaucoup d'immeubles dans une grande ville.

cherry   la cerise

Cherries are red fruit.
Les cerises sont des fruits rouges.

chin   le menton

Jack's chin   **le menton de Jack**

class   la classe

Mr. Levy's class
la classe de monsieur Levy

chick   le poussin

This hen has five chicks.
Cette poule a cinq poussins.

chocolate   le chocolat

a chocolate bar
une tablette de chocolat

classroom   la salle de classe

our classroom   **notre salle de classe**

a b **c** d e f g h i j k l m n o p q r s t u v w x y z

clean¹   **nettoyer**

Clean the glass!   Nettoie la vitre!

clean²   **propre**

Neil has clean clothes.
Neil a des vêtements propres.

climb   **grimper**

Mr. Sparks is climbing the ladder to rescue the cat.
Monsieur Sparks grimpe à l'échelle pour sauver le chat.

clock l'horloge (f), la pendule, (alarm clock) le réveil

My alarm clock is very noisy.
Mon réveil est très bruyant.

close¹   **fermer**

Danny is closing the door.
Danny ferme la porte.

close²   **près**

Bill is close to Ben.
Bill est près de Ben.

clothes   **les vêtements (m)**

clean clothes

des vêtements propres

cloud   **le nuage**

a big, white cloud
un gros nuage blanc

clown   **le clown**

Look, the clown is juggling.
Regarde, le clown jongle.

coat   **le manteau (manteaux)**

Renata has a lovely red coat.
Renata a un beau manteau rouge.

coffee   **le café**

Coffee has a strong taste.
Le café a un goût fort.

coin   **la pièce**

Pete has two coins in his hand.
Pete a deux pièces dans la main.

a b c d e f g h i j k l m n o p q r s t u v w x y z

cold¹   le rhume

Helen has a bad cold.
Helen a un mauvais rhume.

cold²   froid

Ash wears gloves when it's cold.

Ash porte des gants quand il fait froid.

color   la couleur

bright colors   des couleurs vives

green
vert

red
rouge

blue
bleu

yellow
jaune

comb   le peigne

a comb for my hair
un peigne pour mes cheveux

come   venir, arriver

The clown is coming to my party.
Le clown vient à ma fête.

The bus comes at one o'clock.
Le bus arrive à 1 heure.

computer   l'ordinateur (m)

I work on a computer.
Je travaille sur ordinateur.

cook   faire, faire cuire

Dad is cooking pancakes.
Papa fait des crêpes.

copy   copier

Sally's copying what Polly's doing.
Sally copie ce que fait Polly.

country¹   le pays

The map shows the countries of Africa.
La carte montre les pays d'Afrique.

country²   la campagne

springtime in the country

le printemps à la campagne

cow   la vache

Milk comes from cows.
Le lait provient des vaches.

crash   percuter

The car has crashed into the tree.
La voiture a percuté l'arbre.

a b c d e f g h i j k l m n o p q r s t u v w x y z

crawl   marcher à quatre pattes

This baby is crawling.

Ce bébé marche à quatre pattes.

crayon   le crayon cire

a box of crayons
une boîte de crayons cire

creep   se glisser

Anna is creeping into the kitchen.

Anna se glisse dans la cuisine.

crocodile   le crocodile

Crocodiles live near water.
Les crocodiles vivent près de l'eau.

cross[1]   la croix

A cross is made of two lines.

Une croix est composée de deux traits.

cross[2]   traverser

a good place to cross the street

un bon endroit pour traverser la rue

crown   la couronne

Kings and queens wear a crown.
Les rois et les reines portent une couronne.

cry   pleurer

Ross is crying because he has a stomach ache.

Ross pleure parce qu'il a mal au ventre.

cucumber   le concombre

slices of cucumber

des rondelles de concombre

cup   la tasse

I have my tea in a green cup.
Je prends mon thé dans une tasse verte.

cut   couper, (cut out) découper

Danny is cutting a circle.

Danny découpe un cercle.

cycle   aller en vélo

Sara cycles to school.
Sara va à l'école en vélo.

a b c d e f g h i j k l m n o p q r s t u v w x y z

dance — danser

Stef and Laura are dancing together.
Stef et Laura dansent ensemble.

dangerous — dangereux (dangereuse)

a dangerous snake
un serpent dangereux

dark — (night) noir, (color) foncé

It's dark outside.
Il fait noir dehors.

dark blue
bleu foncé

date — la date

What's the date today?
Quelle est la date aujourd'hui?

day — le jour, la journée

The sun shines all day.
Le soleil brille toute la journée.

dear — cher (chère)

Cher Damien
Merci beauc beau cadea envoyé. J'a

Chère Isabelle
Un grand merci pour l'invitation à ta fête le 6 avril.
Je viendrai avec plaisir
Olivia
Bisous

deep — profond

a deep hole
un trou profond

deer — le cerf

Deer live on hills and in woods.
Les cerfs vivent dans les collines et dans les bois.

delicious — délicieux (délicieuse)

Jack's sandwich is delicious.
Le sandwich de Jack est délicieux.

dentist — le or la dentiste

I'm not afraid of the dentist.
Je n'ai pas peur du dentiste.

desert — le désert

Very few plants grow in the desert.
Très peu de plantes poussent dans le désert.

desk — le bureau (bureaux)

My desk has six drawers.
Mon bureau a six tiroirs.

a b c d e f g h i j k l m n o p q r s t u v w x y z

21

dictionary   le dictionnaire

A dictionary can explain what words mean.
Un dictionnaire peut expliquer ce que les mots veulent dire.

USBORNE
PICTURE DICTIONARY

dig   creuser

Anna is digging a hole.
Anna creuse un trou.

dirty   sale

Sally's clothes are very dirty.
Les vêtements de Sally sont très sales.

die   mourir

My plant is dying because of the heat.
Ma plante meurt à cause de la chaleur.

digger   la pelleteuse

a big, yellow digger
une grande pelleteuse jaune

disappear   disparaître

Polly's dog has disappeared.
Le chien de Polly a disparu.

different   différent

The twins wear different colors.
Les jumelles portent des couleurs différentes.

dinner   le dîner

Robert is having his dinner.
Robert prend son dîner.

dive   plonger

Jack is diving into the pool.
Jack plonge dans la piscine.

difficult   difficile

It's difficult to take care of two babies at the same time.
C'est difficile de s'occuper de deux bébés en même temps.

dinosaur   le dinosaure

an enormous dinosaur
un dinosaure énorme

diver   le plongeur

The diver is looking for coral.
Le plongeur cherche du corail.

a b c **d** e f g h i j k l m n o p q r s t u v w x y z

do *to* dream

do   **faire**

Jenny is doing a jigsaw puzzle.
Jenny fait un puzzle.

I'm doing some cooking.
Je fais de la cuisine.

doctor   **le médecin**

The doctor is taking care of Kirsty.
Le médecin s'occupe de Kirsty.

dog   **le chien**

a nice dog   **un chien gentil**

doll   **la poupée**

What's your doll's name?
Comment s'appelle ta poupée?

dolphin   **le dauphin**

A dolphin isn't a fish.
Le dauphin n'est pas un poisson.

donkey   **l'âne (m)**

A donkey looks like a small horse.
Un âne ressemble à un petit cheval.

door   **la porte**

The front door is red.
La porte d'entrée est rouge.

down   **en bas**

This arrow points down.
Cette flèche indique en bas.

dragon   **le dragon**

A dragon is a kind of monster.
Un dragon est une espèce de monstre.

draw   **dessiner**

Molly is drawing a face.
Molly dessine un visage.

drawing   **le dessin**

Here's Molly's drawing.
Voici le dessin de Molly.

dream   **le rêve**

Adam is having a strange dream.
Adam fait un rêve étrange.

a b c **d** e f g h i j k l m n o p q r s t u v w x y z

dress¹   la robe

Anya is wearing a red dress with white flowers.
Anya porte une robe rouge à fleurs blanches.

dress²   s'habiller

Robert is dressing himself.
Robert s'habille.

drink   boire

Polly is drinking orange juice.
Polly boit du jus d'orange.

drive   conduire

Mick is driving a dump truck.
Mick conduit un tombereau.

drop¹   la goutte

two drops of water
deux gouttes d'eau

drop²   laisser tomber

Ellie has dropped her cake.
Ellie a laissé tomber son gâteau.

drum   le tambour

a red drum
un tambour rouge

dry¹   sécher

Anna is drying herself with a blue towel.
Anna se sèche avec une serviette bleue.

dry²   sec (sèche)

The clothes are dry.
Les vêtements sont secs.

duck   le canard

There is a duck on the water.
Il y a un canard sur l'eau.

duckling   le caneton

How many ducklings are there?
Combien de canetons y a-t-il?

dull   (color) **terne,** (story) **sans intérêt**

a dull green
un vert terne

a dull book
un livre sans intérêt

a b c **d** e f g h i j k l m n o p q r s t u v w x y z

Ee
eagle *to* e-mail

eagle — l'aigle (m)

a big, brown eagle
un grand aigle marron

easy — facile

I + I = ?

an easy math problem
un calcul facile

My book is easy to read.
Mon livre est facile à lire.

elbow — le coude

Jack is pointing to his elbow.
Jack indique son coude.

ear — l'oreille (f)

Polly is pointing to Jack's ear.
Polly indique l'oreille de Jack.

eat — manger

Oliver is eating green apples.
Oliver mange des pommes vertes.

electricity — l'électricité (f)

A television needs electricity to work.
Une télévision a besoin d'électricité pour marcher.

early — tôt

Lucy is arriving early at the party.
Lucy arrive tôt à la fête.

edge — le bord

The crayon is on the edge of the table.
Le crayon cire est au bord de la table.

elephant — l'éléphant (m)

an African elephant
un éléphant d'Afrique

earth — la terre

The Earth is our planet.
La Terre est notre planète.

egg — l'œuf (m)

We eat hen's eggs.
Nous mangeons les œufs de poule.

e-mail — l'e-mail (m)

Polly is sending an e-mail.
Polly envoie un e-mail.

a b c d **e** f g h i j k l m n o p q r s t u v w x y z

empty — vide

The cookie jar is empty.
La boîte à biscuits est vide.

envelope — l'enveloppe (f)

a pale green envelope

une enveloppe vert clair

evening — le soir

The sun sets in the evening.

Le soleil se couche le soir.

end — (day, story) la fin, (table, rope) le bout

The End

equal — égal*

The two friends have equal amounts.

Les deux amies ont des quantités égales.

expensive — cher (chère)

The car is more expensive than the duck.

15

4

La voiture est plus chère que le canard.

enjoy — (something) aimer, (yourself) s'amuser

Molly enjoys singing.
Molly aime chanter.
She's enjoying herself.
Elle s'amuse.

escape — s'échapper

The black cat is escaping.
Le chat noir s'échappe.

explain — expliquer

Mr. Levy is explaining these math problems.
Monsieur Levy explique ces calculs.

2+3 =
5+4 =
8+5 =

enormous — énorme

an enormous blue whale
une énorme baleine bleue

even — pair

The pink bunny is jumping on the even numbers.
Le lapin rose saute sur les nombres pairs.

1 2 3 4 5 6 7

eye — l'œil (m) (yeux)

Jack is pointing to Polly's eye.
Jack indique l'oeil de Polly.

a b c d **e** f g h i j k l m n o p q r s t u v w x y z

* masculine plural form: *égaux*

face¹ — le visage, la figure

This is Jack's face.

Voici le visage de Jack *or* Voici la figure de Jack.

face² — faire face

One giraffe is facing the other.

Une girafe fait face à l'autre.

fact — le fait

The fact is that babies sleep a lot.
Le fait est que les bébés dorment beaucoup.

fairy — la fée

This fairy has a magic wand.

Cette fée a une baguette magique.

fall — tomber

When the clown falls, everyone laughs.
Quand le clown tombe, tout le monde rit.

far — loin

The butcher's store isn't far.

La boucherie n'est pas loin.

farm — la ferme

There are sheep on this farm.
Il y a des moutons dans cette ferme.

farmer — le fermier

Mike is a farmer.

Mike est fermier.

fast — vite

Eric goes very fast on his skis.
Eric va très vite sur ses skis.

fat — gros (grosse)

a fat cat
un gros chat

feed — donner à manger

Polly is feeding the hens.

Polly donne à manger aux poules.

feel (touch) **toucher**, (happy or sad) **se sentir**

Feel this silk!
Touche cette soie!

Beth is feeling great.
Beth se sent en forme.

a b c d e f g h i j k l m n o p q r s t u v w x y z

fence la palissade

the backyard fence
la palissade du jardin

few peu

Becky has very few strawberries.
Becky a très peu de fraises.

field le champ

There are some cows in the field.
Il y a des vaches dans le champ.

fight se battre

The children are fighting with cushions.

Les enfants se battent avec des coussins.

fill remplir

Ivan fills his wheelbarrow with sand.
Ivan remplit sa brouette de sable.

find trouver

Megan is finding crayons under the table.
Megan trouve des crayons cire sous la table.

finger le doigt

Jack is pointing to his finger.
Jack indique son doigt.

finish finir

Danny is finishing his drink.
Danny finit sa boisson.

fire le feu (feux), (house on fire) l'incendie (m)

a wood fire
un feu de bois

fire engine la voiture de pompiers

the new fire engine
la voiture de pompiers neuve

firefighter le pompier

Firefighters put out fires.
Les pompiers éteignent les incendies.

first premier (première)

Jenny is first.
Jenny est la première.

a b c d e f g h i j k l m n o p q r s t u v w x y z

28

fish¹   le poisson

I have some tropical fish.
J'ai des poissons tropicaux.

fish²   pêcher

Karl likes fishing.
Karl aime pêcher.

fit¹   être à la taille

This sweater doesn't fit Jenny.
Ce pull n'est pas à la taille de Jenny.

fit²   en forme

Alice plays tennis to keep fit.
Alice joue au tennis pour se maintenir en forme.

fix   réparer

Eve is fixing her doll.
Eve répare sa poupée.

flag   le drapeau (drapeaux)

the French flag
le drapeau de la France

flat   plat

A board is a flat piece of wood.
Une planche est un morceau de bois plat.

float   flotter

The yellow duck is floating.
Le canard jaune flotte.

flood   l'inondation (f)

There are often floods here.
Il y a souvent des inondations ici.

floor   la terre

There are lots of toys on the floor.

Il y a beaucoup de jouets par terre.

flour   la farine

Here's some flour for making bread.
Voici de la farine pour faire du pain.

flower   la fleur

Roses are my favorite flowers.
Les roses sont mes fleurs préférées.

a b c d e **f** g h i j k l m n o p q r s t u v w x y z

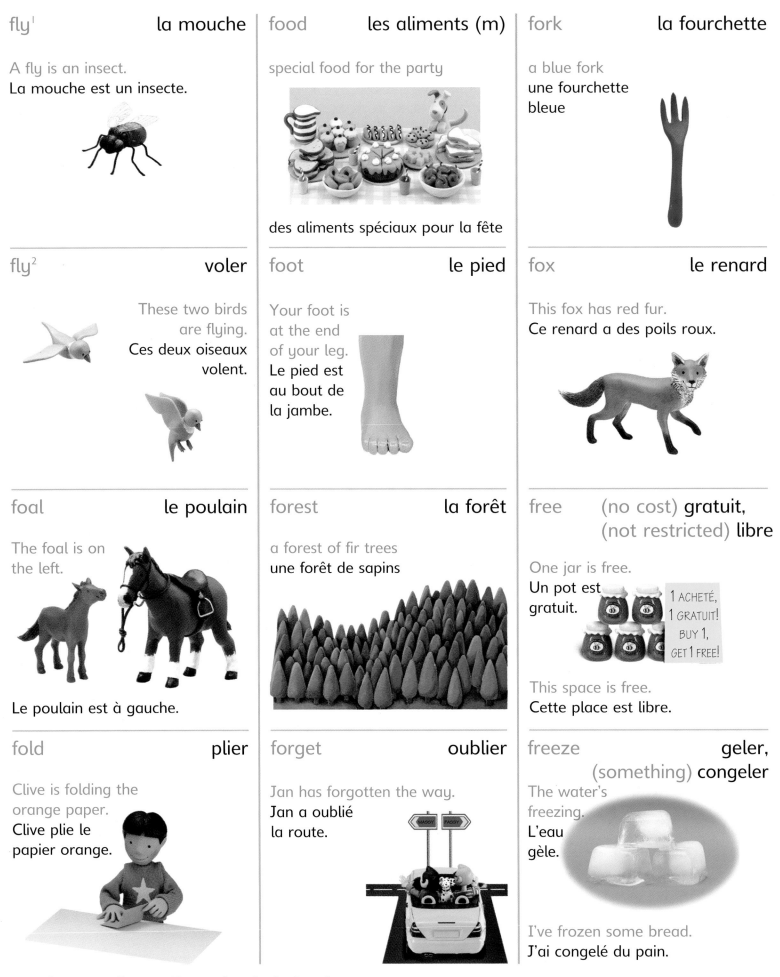

fly¹   la mouche

A fly is an insect.
La mouche est un insecte.

fly²   voler

These two birds
are flying.
Ces deux oiseaux
volent.

foal   le poulain

The foal is on
the left.

Le poulain est à gauche.

fold   plier

Clive is folding the
orange paper.
Clive plie le
papier orange.

food   les aliments (m)

special food for the party

des aliments spéciaux pour la fête

foot   le pied

Your foot is
at the end
of your leg.
Le pied est
au bout de
la jambe.

forest   la forêt

a forest of fir trees
une forêt de sapins

forget   oublier

Jan has forgotten the way.
Jan a oublié
la route.

fork   la fourchette

a blue fork
une fourchette
bleue

fox   le renard

This fox has red fur.
Ce renard a des poils roux.

free   (no cost) gratuit,
          (not restricted) libre

One jar is free.
Un pot est
gratuit.

1 ACHETÉ,
1 GRATUIT!
BUY 1,
GET 1 FREE!

This space is free.
Cette place est libre.

freeze   geler,
       (something) congeler

The water's
freezing.
L'eau
gèle.

I've frozen some bread.
J'ai congelé du pain.

a b c d e f g h i j k l m n o p q r s t u v w x y z

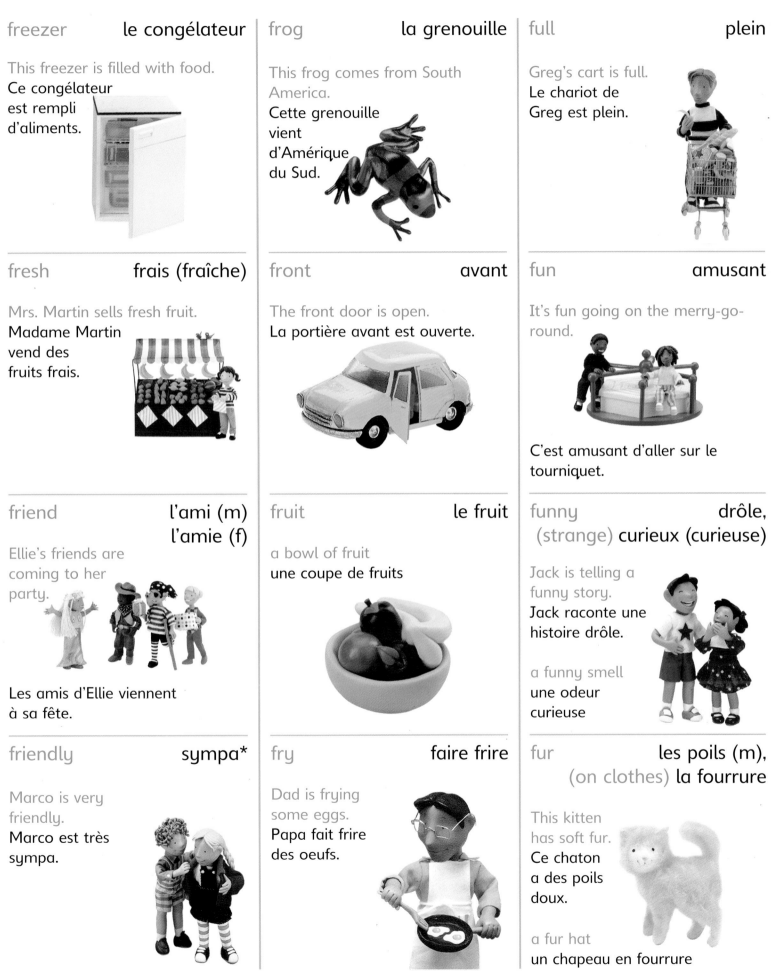

freezer   le congélateur

This freezer is filled with food.
Ce congélateur est rempli d'aliments.

fresh   frais (fraîche)

Mrs. Martin sells fresh fruit.
Madame Martin vend des fruits frais.

friend   l'ami (m) l'amie (f)

Ellie's friends are coming to her party.
Les amis d'Ellie viennent à sa fête.

friendly   sympa*

Marco is very friendly.
Marco est très sympa.

frog   la grenouille

This frog comes from South America.
Cette grenouille vient d'Amérique du Sud.

front   avant

The front door is open.
La portière avant est ouverte.

fruit   le fruit

a bowl of fruit
une coupe de fruits

fry   faire frire

Dad is frying some eggs.
Papa fait frire des oeufs.

full   plein

Greg's cart is full.
Le chariot de Greg est plein.

fun   amusant

It's fun going on the merry-go-round.
C'est amusant d'aller sur le tourniquet.

funny   drôle, (strange) curieux (curieuse)

Jack is telling a funny story.
Jack raconte une histoire drôle.

a funny smell
une odeur curieuse

fur   les poils (m), (on clothes) la fourrure

This kitten has soft fur.
Ce chaton a des poils doux.

a fur hat
un chapeau en fourrure

a b c d e f g h i j k l m n o p q r s t u v w x y z

* "sympa" is short for "sympathique", and it is the same for both masculine and feminine.

game   **le jeu (jeux)**

a game of basketball
un jeu de basket

gentle   **doux (douce)**

Pip is a gentle dog.
Pip est un chien doux.

gift   **le cadeau (cadeaux)**

Becky has a gift for Polly's birthday.
Becky a un cadeau pour l'anniversaire de Polly.

garden   **le jardin**

There are lots of flowers in Aggie's garden.
Il y a beaucoup de fleurs dans le jardin d'Aggie.

gerbil   **la gerbille**

A gerbil is a small animal.
La gerbille est un petit animal.

giraffe   **la girafe**

A giraffe is an African animal.
La girafe est un animal d'Afrique.

gas   **le gaz**

This balloon is filled with gas.
Ce ballon est gonflé au gaz.

ghost   **le fantôme**

I don't believe in ghosts.
Je ne crois pas aux fantômes.

girl   **la fille**

three little girls
trois petites filles

gate   **la barrière**

The yard has a blue gate.
Le jardin a une barrière bleue.

giant   **le géant**

a friendly giant
un géant sympa

give   **donner**

Ethan is giving Jenny some wagons.
Ethan donne des wagons à Jenny.

a b c d e f **g** h i j k l m n o p q r s t u v w x y z

glad — content

Sally is glad to see Jenny.
Sally est contente de voir Jenny.

glass — le verre

a glass of milk
un verre de lait

Windows are made with glass.
Les fenêtres sont fabriquées avec du verre.

glasses — les lunettes (f)

Dad and Grandma wear glasses.
Papa et Mamie portent des lunettes.

glove — le gant

Polly has some red gloves.
Polly a des gants rouges.

glue — la colle

Danny is making a picture with paper and glue.
Danny fait un tableau avec du papier et de la colle.

go — aller

The cars are going into the ferry.
Les voitures vont dans le car-ferry.

goal — le but

Our team has scored a goal.
Notre équipe a marqué un but.

BUT!

goat — la chèvre

Goats climb hills very well.
Les chèvres grimpent très bien dans les collines.

gold — l'or (m), (golden) doré

Gold is a precious metal.
L'or est un métal précieux.

good — bon (bonne), (well done) bien fait, (child) sage

a good meal
un bon repas

This is good work.
Voici du travail bien fait.

3 + 3 = 6 ✓
2 + 5 = 7 ✓
8 - 6 = 2 ✓
4 + 1 = 5 ✓

Be good!
Sois sage!

goodbye — au revoir

Polly is saying goodbye to her friends.
Polly dit au revoir à ses amis.

Au revoir!

goose — l'oie (f)

There are often geese on farms.
Il y a souvent des oies à la ferme.

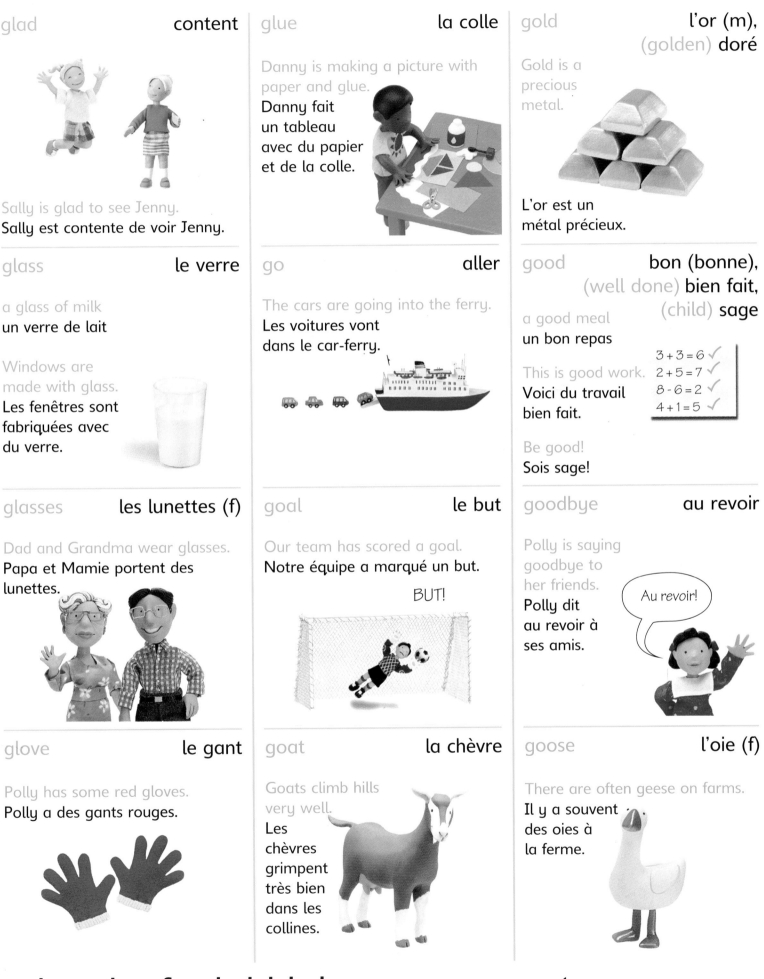

a b c d e f **g** h i j k l m n o p q r s t u v w x y z

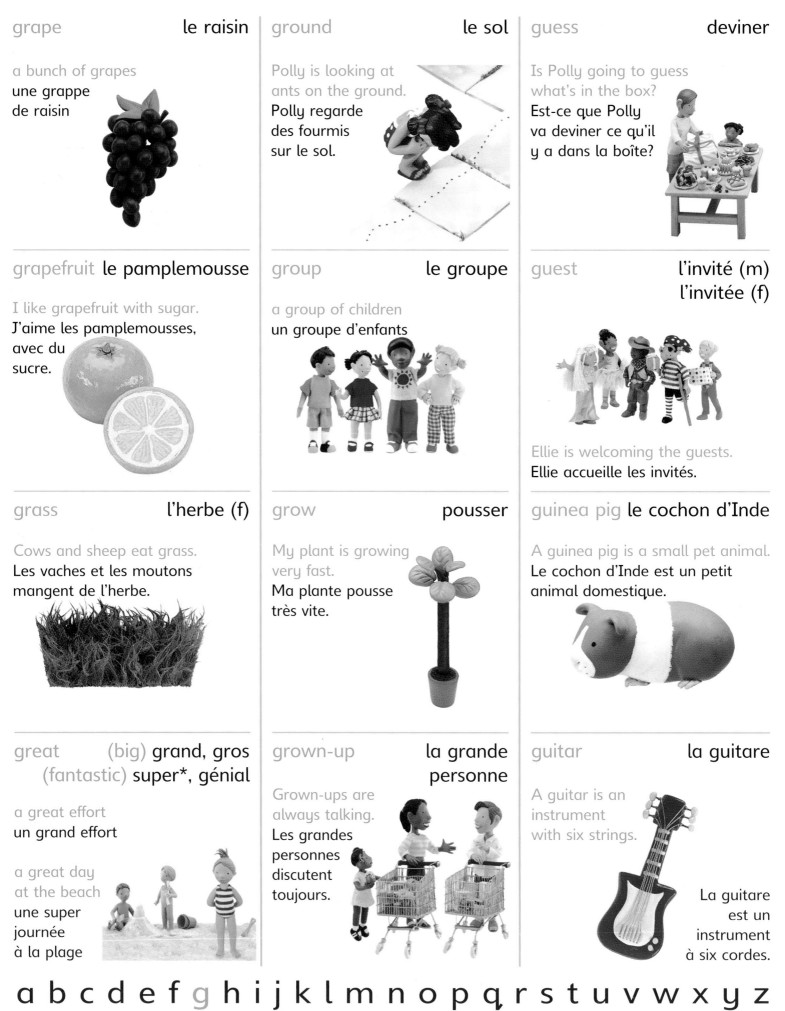

grape   le raisin

a bunch of grapes
une grappe
de raisin

ground   le sol

Polly is looking at
ants on the ground.
Polly regarde
des fourmis
sur le sol.

guess   deviner

Is Polly going to guess
what's in the box?
Est-ce que Polly
va deviner ce qu'il
y a dans la boîte?

grapefruit   le pamplemousse

I like grapefruit with sugar.
J'aime les pamplemousses,
avec du
sucre.

group   le groupe

a group of children
un groupe d'enfants

guest   l'invité (m)
l'invitée (f)

Ellie is welcoming the guests.
Ellie accueille les invités.

grass   l'herbe (f)

Cows and sheep eat grass.
Les vaches et les moutons
mangent de l'herbe.

grow   pousser

My plant is growing
very fast.
Ma plante pousse
très vite.

guinea pig   le cochon d'Inde

A guinea pig is a small pet animal.
Le cochon d'Inde est un petit
animal domestique.

great   (big) grand, gros
(fantastic) super*, génial

a great effort
un grand effort

a great day
at the beach
une super
journée
à la plage

grown-up   la grande
personne

Grown-ups are
always talking.
Les grandes
personnes
discutent
toujours.

guitar   la guitare

A guitar is an
instrument
with six strings.

La guitare
est un
instrument
à six cordes.

a b c d e f **g** h i j k l m n o p q r s t u v w x y z
* "super" is the same for both masculine and feminine.

Hh hair *to* hard

hair — les cheveux (m)

Rosie and Katie have fair hair.
Rosie et Katie ont les cheveux blonds.

hairbrush — la brosse

I have a red hairbrush.
J'ai une brosse rouge.

half — le demi, la demie, (portion) la moitié

one and a half hours
une heure et demie

half the bun
la moitié du petit pain

hamburger — le hamburger

Dad's making hamburgers.
Papa fait des hamburgers.

hammer — le marteau (marteaux)

a hammer for doing carpentry
un marteau pour faire du bricolage

hamster — le hamster

Hamsters eat nuts and seeds.
Les hamsters mangent des noix et des graines.

hand — la main

This is Jack's left hand.
Voici la main gauche de Jack.

handle — (door) la clenche, (knife, pan) le manche

a door handle
une clenche de porte

The pan handle's broken.
Le manche de la poêle est cassée.

hang — pendre, (put up) accrocher

Jack is hanging his jacket.
Jack pend son blouson.

Polly's hanging decorations.
Polly accroche des décorations.

happen — arriver, se passer

What's happening here?
Qu'est-ce qu'il se passe ici?

happy — content, heureux (heureuse)

Sally is feeling very happy today.
Sally se sent très heureuse aujourd'hui.

hard — dur

a hard job
un travail dur

hard ground
un sol dur

a b c d e f g **h** i j k l m n o p q r s t u v w x y z

hat   le chapeau (chapeaux)

I have an orange hat with a flower.

J'ai un chapeau orange avec une fleur.

hate   détester

Maddy hates spiders.

Maddy déteste les araignées.

have   avoir

Julia has some new red shoes.
Julia a des chaussures rouges neuves.

Poor Helen has a cold.
La pauvre Helen a un rhume.

head   la tête

Polly's head is in the circle.
La tête de Polly est dans le cercle.

hear   entendre

Jack can hear the dog barking.

Wouah wouah!

Jack entend le chien qui aboie.

heart   le cœur

My heart is beating fast.
Mon cœur bat vite.

heart shaped
en forme de cœur

heat   chauffer

Yvonne is heating coffee in the microwave.
Yvonne chauffe du café dans le micro-ondes.

heavy   lourd

The boys are trying to move a heavy package.

Les garçons essaient de déplacer un paquet lourd.

height   la taille

Dad is checking Milo's height.
Papa vérifie la taille de Milo.

helicopter   l'hélicoptère (m)

an emergency helicopter
un hélicoptère des secours

hello   bonjour, (to friends) salut

Lisa is saying hello to her sister.

Salut!

Lisa dit bonjour à sa sœur.

helmet   le casque

Grace wears a helmet for skateboarding.
Grace porte un casque pour faire de la planche à roulettes.

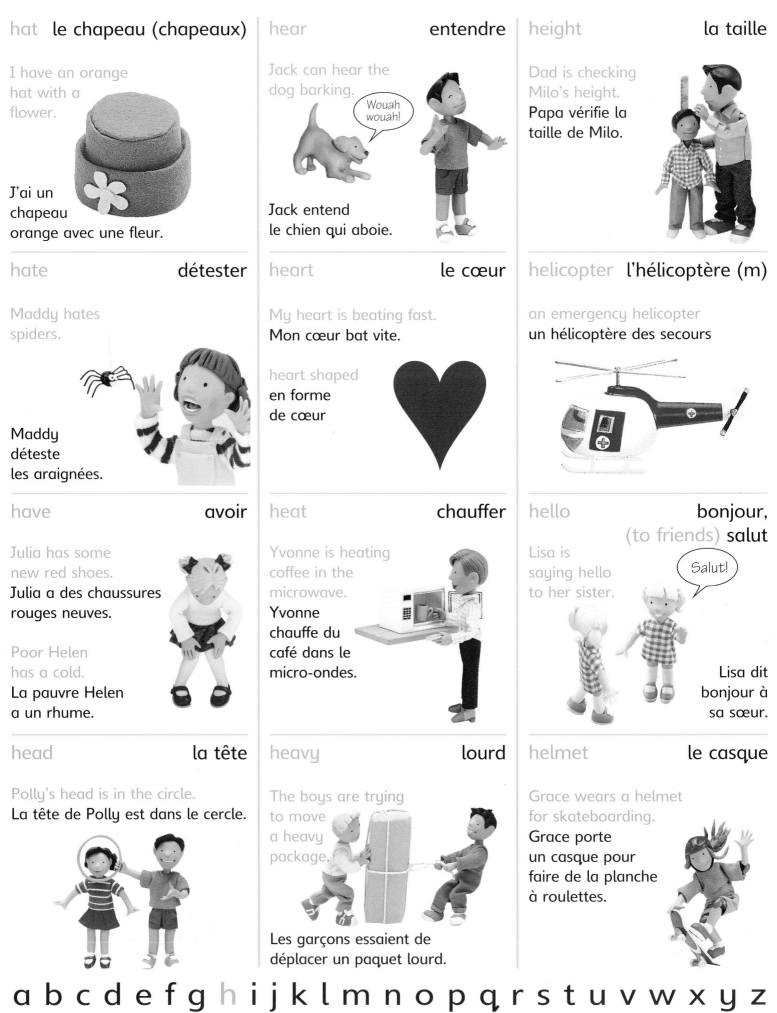

a b c d e f g **h** i j k l m n o p q r s t u v w x y z

36

help — aider

Jack is helping his dad with the cooking.
Jack aide son papa à la cuisine.

highchair — la chaise haute

Small children have highchairs.
Les petits enfants ont des chaises hautes.

hold — (in your hands) tenir, (contain) contenir

Neil is holding the trophy.
Neil tient la coupe.

How many does the box hold?
Combien contient la boîte?

hen — la poule

Most eggs come from hens.

La plupart des œufs proviennent des poules.

hill — la colline

The house is at the top of the hill.
La maison est au sommet de la colline.

hole — le trou

There's a hole in this sweater.
Il y a un trou dans ce pull.

hide — (things) cacher, (yourself) se cacher

The clown is hiding behind the armchair.
Le clown se cache derrière le fauteuil.

hippopotamus *or* hippo — l'hippopotame (m)

Hippos live in Africa.

Les hippopotames vivent en Afrique.

home — la maison

This is our home.

Voici notre maison.

high — haut

The balloon is high in the sky.
La montgolfière est très haut dans le ciel.

a high building
un immeuble haut

hit — frapper

Alice is hitting the ball with her racket.
Alice frappe la balle avec sa raquette.

honey — le miel

Honey is very sweet.
Le miel est très sucré.

a b c d e f g **h** i j k l m n o p q r s t u v w x y z

hop sauter à cloche-pied

Anna is hopping.

Anna saute à cloche-pied.

horse le cheval (chevaux)

Martin's horse is named Star.

Le cheval de Martin s'appelle Star.

hospital l'hôpital (m) (hôpitaux)

This is the new hospital.

Voici le nouvel hôpital.

hot chaud

Careful, it's hot!

Attention, c'est chaud!

hotdog le hot-dog

A hotdog is a sausage on a bun.

Un hot-dog est une saucisse avec un petit pain.

hotel l'hôtel (m)

Mr. Brand is spending his vacation at this hotel.

Monsieur Brand passe ses vacances dans cet hôtel.

HOTEL LUCIDA

hour l'heure (f)

The little hand on a clock shows the hours.

La petite aiguille de l'horloge indique les heures.

house la maison

a family house une maison de famille

hug embrasser

Nicholas is hugging his teddy bear.

Nicholas embrasse son nounours.

(to be) hungry avoir faim

Oliver is very hungry.

Oliver a très faim.

hurry se dépêcher

Jack and Polly are hurrying to catch the dog.

Jack et Polly se dépêchent pour rattraper le chien.

hurt faire mal

Ow! It hurts!

Aïe! Ça fait mal!

a b c d e f g **h** i j k l m n o p q r s t u v w x y z

Ii ice *to* itch

ice   la glace, (cube) le glaçon

snow and ice
la neige et la glace

water with ice
de l'eau avec des glaçons

ice cream   la glace

different flavors of ice cream
de la glace à différents parfums

idea   l'idée (f)

Allons jouer au parc!

Andy has an idea: Let's go and play in the park!

Andy a une idée.

insect   l'insecte (m)

All insects have six legs.

Tous les insectes ont six pattes.

inside   à l'intérieur, (in) dans

The kitten is inside the flowerpot.
Le chaton est à l'intérieur du pot de fleurs or dans le pot de fleurs.

Let's stay inside.
Restons à l'intérieur.

instead   au lieu

J'ai fait du thé glacé au lieu de jus de fruits aujourd'hui.

Mrs. Dot has made iced tea instead of fruit juice today.

Internet   Internet (m)

Polly is searching the Internet.
Polly fait des recherches sur Internet.

invitation   l'invitation (f)

a party invitation   une invitation à la fête

Isabelle t'invite à sa Fête d'anniversaire le samedi 6 avril à 4 heures RSVP

invite   inviter

Imogen is inviting Martin to her party.

Est-ce que tu veux venir à ma fête?

Imogen invite Martin à sa fête.

iron   le fer (à repasser)

This is a steam iron.
Voici un fer à vapeur.

island   l'île (f)

a desert island
une île déserte

itch   démanger

Fred's ear itches.
L'oreille de Fred le démange.

a b c d e f g h i j k l m n o p q r s t u v w x y z

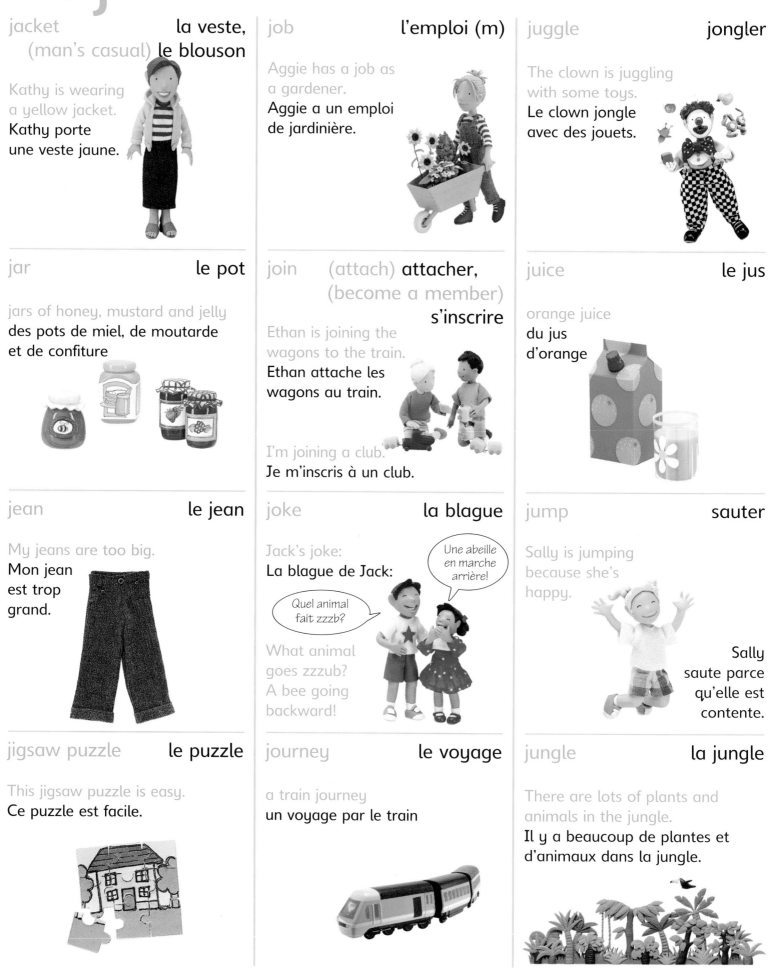

jacket (man's casual)
la veste, le blouson

Kathy is wearing a yellow jacket.
Kathy porte une veste jaune.

jar **le pot**

jars of honey, mustard and jelly
des pots de miel, de moutarde et de confiture

jean **le jean**

My jeans are too big.
Mon jean est trop grand.

jigsaw puzzle **le puzzle**

This jigsaw puzzle is easy.
Ce puzzle est facile.

job **l'emploi (m)**

Aggie has a job as a gardener.
Aggie a un emploi de jardinière.

join (attach) **attacher,** (become a member) **s'inscrire**

Ethan is joining the wagons to the train.
Ethan attache les wagons au train.

I'm joining a club.
Je m'inscris à un club.

joke **la blague**

Jack's joke:
La blague de Jack:

Quel animal fait zzzb?

Une abeille en marche arrière!

What animal goes zzzub?
A bee going backward!

journey **le voyage**

a train journey
un voyage par le train

juggle **jongler**

The clown is juggling with some toys.
Le clown jongle avec des jouets.

juice **le jus**

orange juice
du jus d'orange

jump **sauter**

Sally is jumping because she's happy.

Sally saute parce qu'elle est contente.

jungle **la jungle**

There are lots of plants and animals in the jungle.
Il y a beaucoup de plantes et d'animaux dans la jungle.

a b c d e f g h i **j** k l m n o p q r s t u v w x y z

Kk kangaroo *to* kite

kangaroo le kangourou

A kangaroo is an Australian animal.
Le kangourou est un animal d'Australie.

kid le chevreau (chevreaux)

a goat and her kid
une chèvre et son chevreau

king le roi

Adam is dressed up as a king.
Adam est déguisé en roi.

keep garder

Sam keeps his things on the shelf.
Sam garde ses affaires sur l'étagère.

I'm keeping supper hot.
Je garde le diner chaud.

kill tuer

The heat has killed my plant.
La chaleur a tué ma plante.

kiss donner un baiser

Polly is kissing Alex.
Polly donne un baiser à Alex.

key la clé, la clef

the front door key
la clé de la porte d'entrée *or* la clef de la porte d'entrée

kind¹ l'espèce (f)

different kinds of fruit
différentes espèces de fruits

kitchen la cuisine

Dad and Jack are in the kitchen.
Papa et Jack sont dans la cuisine.

kick donner un coup de pied

Neil is kicking the ball.
Neil donne un coup de pied dans le ballon.

kind² gentil (gentille)

Mr. Dot is kind. He does his neighbor's shopping.
Monsieur Dot est gentil. Il fait les courses pour son voisin.

kite le cerf-volant

a red and yellow kite
un cerf-volant rouge et jaune

a b c d e f g h i j k l m n o p q r s t u v w x y z

41

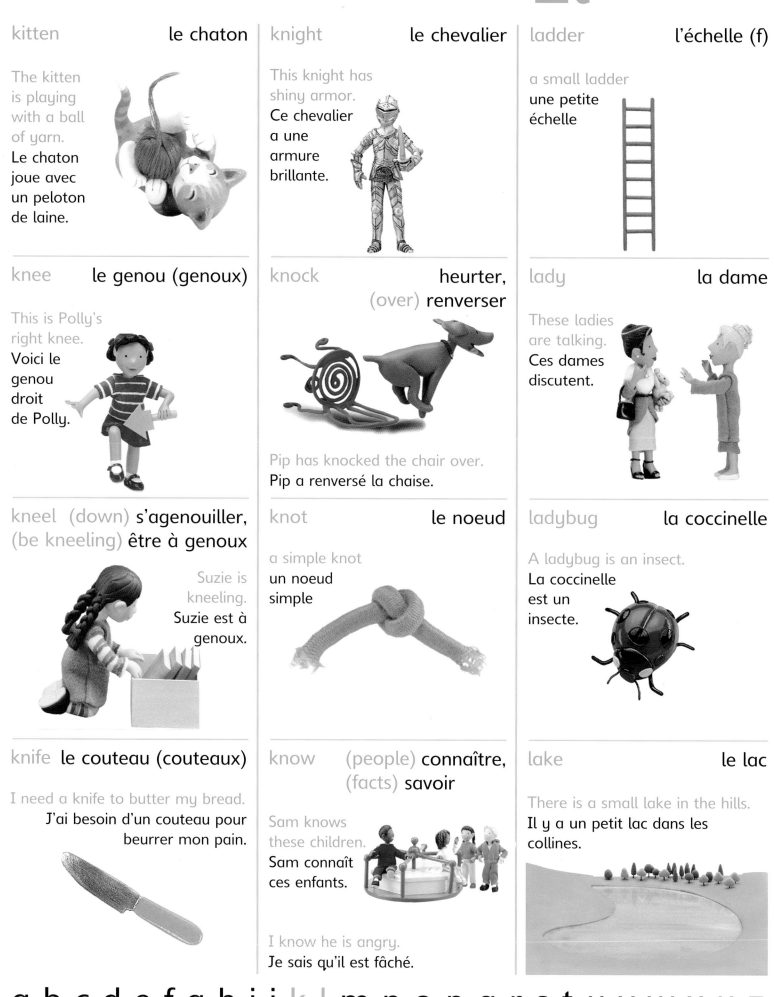

kitten — le chaton

The kitten is playing with a ball of yarn.
Le chaton joue avec un peloton de laine.

knight — le chevalier

This knight has shiny armor.
Ce chevalier a une armure brillante.

ladder — l'échelle (f)

a small ladder
une petite échelle

knee — le genou (genoux)

This is Polly's right knee.
Voici le genou droit de Polly.

knock — heurter, (over) renverser

Pip has knocked the chair over.
Pip a renversé la chaise.

lady — la dame

These ladies are talking.
Ces dames discutent.

kneel (down) s'agenouiller, (be kneeling) être à genoux

Suzie is kneeling.
Suzie est à genoux.

knot — le noeud

a simple knot
un noeud simple

ladybug — la coccinelle

A ladybug is an insect.
La coccinelle est un insecte.

knife le couteau (couteaux)

I need a knife to butter my bread.
J'ai besoin d'un couteau pour beurrer mon pain.

know (people) connaître, (facts) savoir

Sam knows these children.
Sam connaît ces enfants.

I know he is angry.
Je sais qu'il est fâché.

lake — le lac

There is a small lake in the hills.
Il y a un petit lac dans les collines.

a b c d e f g h i j k l m n o p q r s t u v w x y z

lamb   l'agneau (m) (agneaux)

A lamb is a baby sheep.
L'agneau est un bébé mouton.

lamp   la lampe

Here are two small lamps.
Voici deux petites lampes.

land   la terre

On this map, the land is in brown.
Sur cette carte, la terre est en marron.

language   le langage, (foreign) la langue

Guten Tag!

¡Buenos días!

They can speak foreign languages.
Ils parlent des langues étrangères.

large   grand, gros (grosse)

Becky is under a large tree.
Becky est sous un grand arbre.

last   dernier (dernière)

The black dog is last.
Le chien noir est le dernier.

late (not on time) **en retard,** (near the end) **tard**

The bus is always late.
Le bus est toujours en retard.

late at night
tard dans la nuit

laugh   rire

Jack and Polly are laughing.

Ah ha ha

Hi hi hi

Jack et Polly rient.

lazy   paresseux (paresseuse)

a lazy cat
un chat paresseux

lead   mener

The duck is leading her ducklings.

La cane mène ses canetons.

This road leads to the village.
Cette route mène au village.

leaf   la feuille

leaves from a tree

des feuilles d'arbre

lean   pencher, (people) se pencher

the Leaning Tower of Pisa
la Tour penchée de Pise

a b c d e f g h i j k l m n o p q r s t u v w x y z

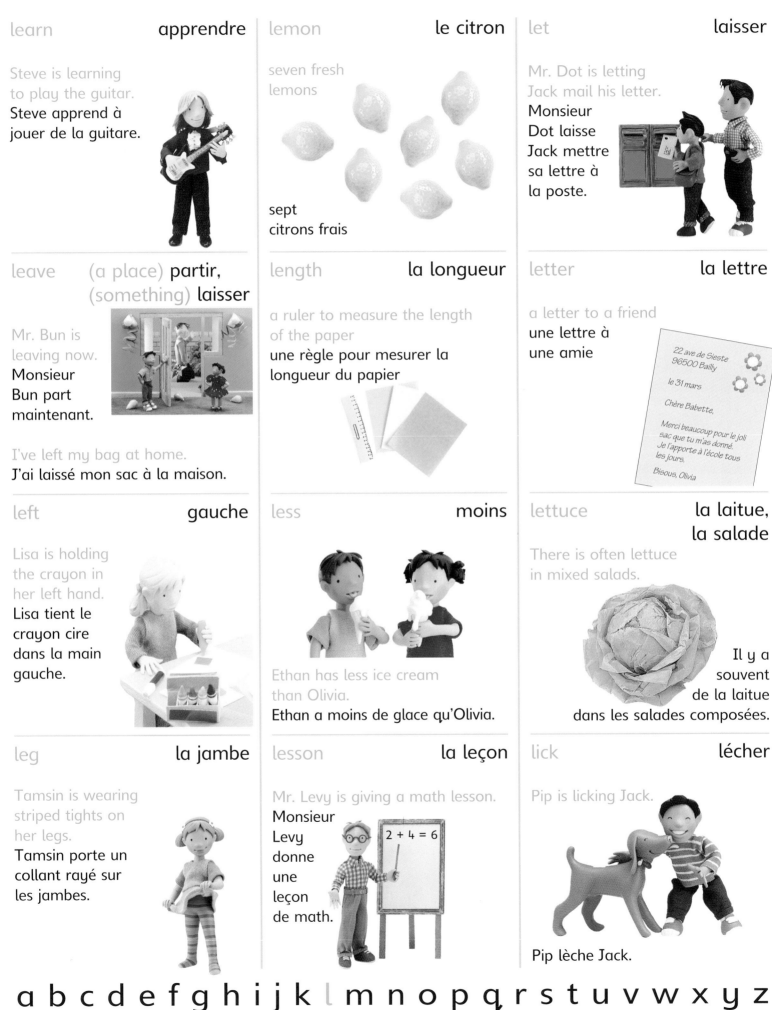

learn   **apprendre**

Steve is learning
to play the guitar.
Steve apprend à
jouer de la guitare.

leave   (a place) **partir,**
(something) **laisser**

Mr. Bun is
leaving now.
Monsieur
Bun part
maintenant.

I've left my bag at home.
J'ai laissé mon sac à la maison.

left   **gauche**

Lisa is holding
the crayon in
her left hand.
Lisa tient le
crayon cire
dans la main
gauche.

leg   **la jambe**

Tamsin is wearing
striped tights on
her legs.
Tamsin porte un
collant rayé sur
les jambes.

lemon   **le citron**

seven fresh
lemons

sept
citrons frais

length   **la longueur**

a ruler to measure the length
of the paper
une règle pour mesurer la
longueur du papier

less   **moins**

Ethan has less ice cream
than Olivia.
Ethan a moins de glace qu'Olivia.

lesson   **la leçon**

Mr. Levy is giving a math lesson.
Monsieur
Levy
donne
une
leçon
de math.

let   **laisser**

Mr. Dot is letting
Jack mail his letter.
Monsieur
Dot laisse
Jack mettre
sa lettre à
la poste.

letter   **la lettre**

a letter to a friend
une lettre à
une amie

22 ave de Sieste
96500 Bailly

le 31 mars

Chère Babette,

Merci beaucoup pour le joli
sac que tu m'as donné.
Je l'apporte à l'école tous
les jours.

Bisous, Olivia

lettuce   **la laitue,**
la salade

There is often lettuce
in mixed salads.

Il y a
souvent
de la laitue
dans les salades composées.

lick   **lécher**

Pip is licking Jack.

Pip lèche Jack.

a b c d e f g h i j k l m n o p q r s t u v w x y z

lid **le couvercle**

the lid of the mustard jar
le couvercle du pot de moutarde

lie[1] (lie down) **se coucher,** (be lying) **être couché**

Kirsty is lying in bed.
Kirsty est couchée dans son lit.

lie[2] **mentir**

Oliver is lying. **Oliver ment.**

Elle n'est pas là? *Non!*

life **la vie**

Grandma and Granddad have had long, happy lives.
Mamie et Papi ont eu une longue vie heureuse.

lift **soulever**

The clown is lifting a tree.
Le clown soulève un arbre.

light[1] **la lumière**

This lamp gives a lot of light.
Cette lampe donne beaucoup de lumière.

Switch off the lights!
Éteignez la lumière!

light[2] (color) **clair,** (not heavy) **léger (légère)**

light pink
rose clair

light as a feather
léger comme une plume

like[1] **aimer**

Becky likes strawberries.
Becky aime les fraises.

like[2] **comme**

Sara has black hair, like her brother.
Sara a les cheveux noirs, comme son frère.

line (in drawing) **le trait,** (of people) **la rangée, la file**

a line of soccer players
une rangée de joueurs de foot

lion **le lion**

A lion is a wild animal.
Le lion est un animal sauvage.

lip **la lèvre**

Zach's top lip
la lèvre supérieure de Zach

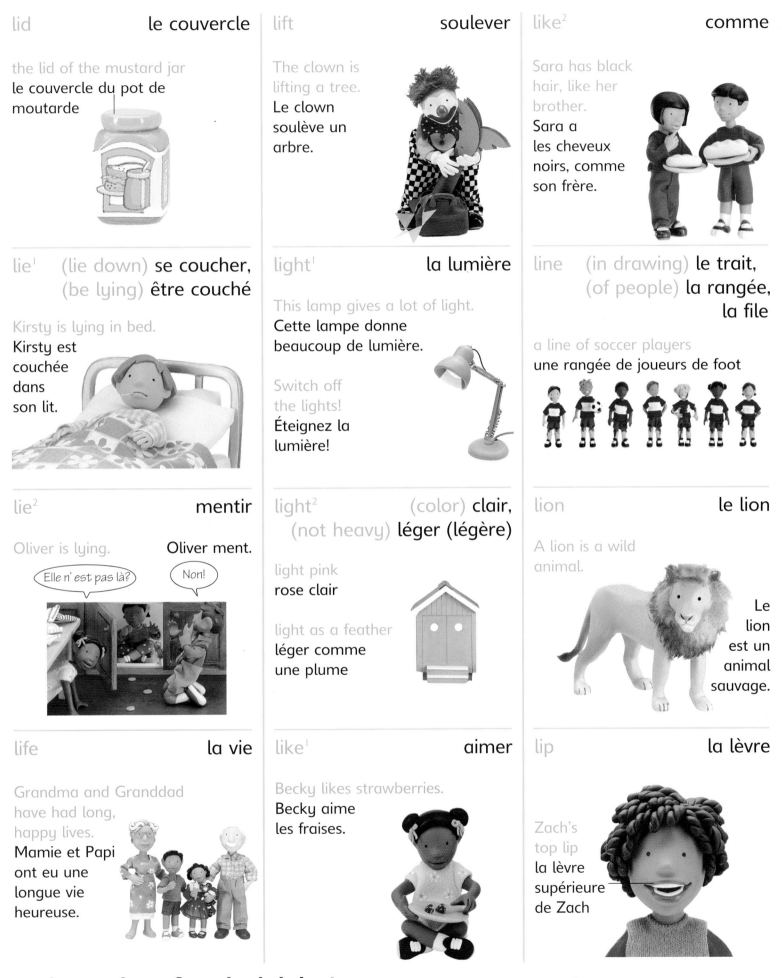

a b c d e f g h i j k l m n o p q r s t u v w x y z

list — **la liste**

a list of first names
une liste de prénoms

Adam
Becky
Danny
Ellie
Katie
Maddy
Ross
Tony

long — **long (longue)**

A giraffe has a very long neck.
La girafe a un cou très long.

loud — **fort**

The music is very loud.
La musique est très forte.

live — **(in a place) habiter, (be alive) vivre**

The Dot family lives here.
La famille Dot habite ici.

look — **regarder**

Polly is looking at the clown.
Polly regarde le clown.

love — **(people) aimer, (things) adorer**

Beth loves taking a bath.
Beth adore prendre son bain.

lock — **la serrure**

I need the key for this lock.
J'ai besoin de la clé de cette serrure.

lose — **perdre**

I've lost my ticket.
J'ai perdu mon billet.

The boys have lost the match.
Les garçons ont perdu la partie.

low — **bas (basse)**

This bird is flying very low.
Cet oiseau vole très bas.

log — **la bûche**

a log for the fire
une bûche pour le feu

(a) lot — **beaucoup**

a lot of teddy bears
beaucoup de nounours

lunch — **le déjeuner**

Sally is eating pizza for lunch.
Sally mange de la pizza pour son déjeuner.

a b c d e f g h i j k l m n o p q r s t u v w x y z

machine **la machine**

a sewing machine

une machine à coudre

magic **la magie**

The clown is doing some magic.
Le clown fait de
la magie.

main **principal***

the main
entrance of
the museum
l'entrée
principale
du musée

make **faire**

Ethan is making a
potato person.
Ethan fait un
bonhomme avec
une pomme
de terre.

man **l'homme (m)**

This man has
black hair.
Cet homme
a les cheveux
noirs.

many **beaucoup**

There are
many
bees
on this
flower.

Il y a
beaucoup
d'abeilles sur
cette fleur.

map **la carte**

a map of the region
une carte de la région

market **le marché**

the fruit and vegetable market
le marché des fruits et légumes

match¹ (game) **le match,**
la partie,
(for fire) **l'allumette (f)**

a soccer match
un match de foot

I have only
one match
Je n'ai qu'une
allumette

match² **faire la paire,**
être assorti

These socks match.
Ces chaussettes
font la paire.

These socks
don't match.
Ces chaussettes
ne font pas
la paire.

matter **être important**

Winning matters a lot to Neil and
his team.

Gagner, c'est très important pour
Neil et son équipe.

meal **le repas**

The meal is ready.
Le repas est prêt.

a b c d e f g h i j k l m n o p q r s t u v w x y z

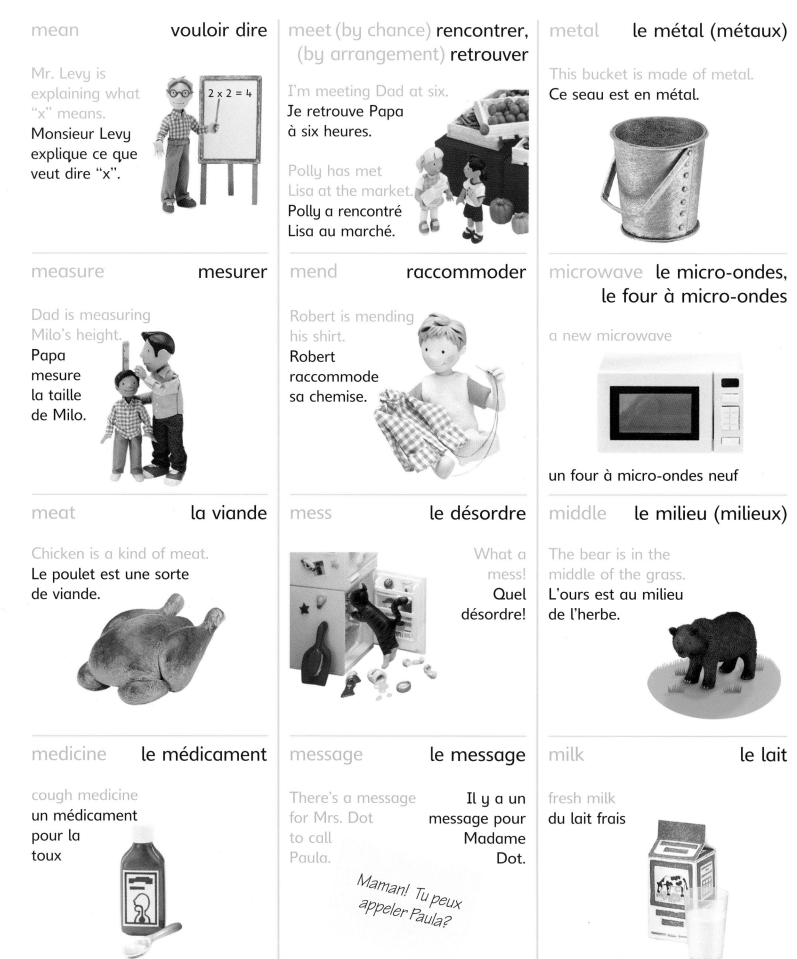

mean   vouloir dire

Mr. Levy is explaining what "x" means.
Monsieur Levy explique ce que veut dire "x".

2 x 2 = 4

meet (by chance) rencontrer, (by arrangement) **retrouver**

I'm meeting Dad at six.
Je retrouve Papa à six heures.

Polly has met Lisa at the market.
Polly a rencontré Lisa au marché.

metal   le métal (métaux)

This bucket is made of metal.
Ce seau est en métal.

measure   mesurer

Dad is measuring Milo's height.
Papa mesure la taille de Milo.

mend   raccommoder

Robert is mending his shirt.
Robert raccommode sa chemise.

microwave le micro-ondes, le four à micro-ondes

a new microwave

un four à micro-ondes neuf

meat   la viande

Chicken is a kind of meat.
Le poulet est une sorte de viande.

mess   le désordre

What a mess!
Quel désordre!

middle le milieu (milieux)

The bear is in the middle of the grass.
L'ours est au milieu de l'herbe.

medicine   le médicament

cough medicine
un médicament pour la toux

message   le message

There's a message for Mrs. Dot to call Paula.
Il y a un message pour Madame Dot.

Maman! Tu peux appeler Paula?

milk   le lait

fresh milk
du lait frais

a b c d e f g h i j k l **m** n o p q r s t u v w x y z

mind — déranger*

I don't mind spiders.
Les araignées ne me dérangent pas.

mistake — la faute

I've made a mistake.
J'ai fait une faute.

chocolat
coccinelle
dinosaure
girafe
hélicoptère

monkey — le singe

five funny monkeys
cinq drôles de singes

minute — la minute

It's a few minutes past nine.
Il est 9 heures et quelques minutes.

mix — mélanger

Oliver is mixing the ingredients to make a cake.
Oliver mélange les ingrédients pour faire un gâteau.

month — le mois

There are twelve months.
Il y a douze mois.

Janvier												
Février												
Mars												
Avril												
Mai												
Juin												
Juillet												
Août												
Septembre												
Octobre												
Novembre												
Décembre												

mirror — le miroir

Jack's looking at himself in the mirror.
Jack se regarde dans le miroir.

model — le modèle, le modèle réduit

Billy is playing with a model.
Billy joue avec un modèle réduit.

moon — la lune

Look at the moon!
Regarde la lune!

miss (someone) — manquer*, (not catch or hit) rater

Liddy misses her mom.
La maman de Liddy lui manque.

Becky's missed the bus.
Becky a raté le bus.

money — l'argent (m)

I have some money for my lunch.
J'ai de l'argent pour mon déjeuner.

more — plus

Sally has more sand than Amy.

Sally   Amy

Sally a plus de sable qu'Amy.

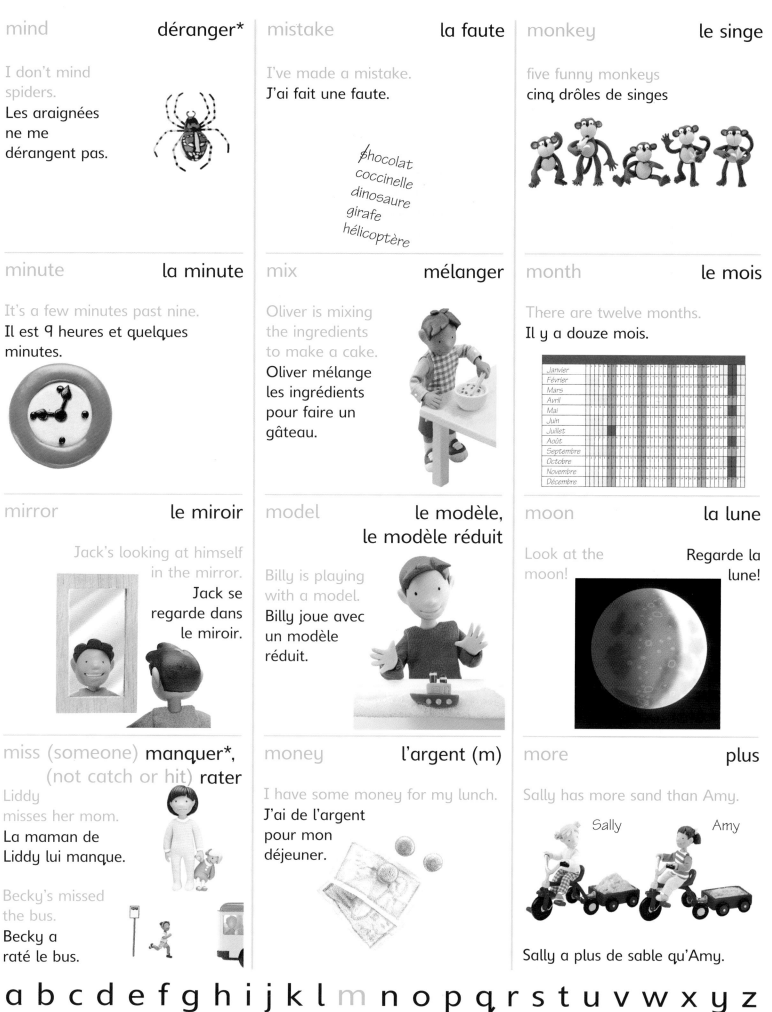

a b c d e f g h i j k l m n o p q r s t u v w x y z

* These two verbs are the other way around from English – as though you were saying "Spiders don't bother me".

morning **le matin**

a fine summer morning
un beau matin d'été

mountain **la montagne**

Mountains are higher than hills.
Les montagnes sont plus hautes
que les collines.

much **beaucoup**

Mrs. Moon hasn't done much shopping.
Madame Moon n'a pas fait beaucoup de courses.

most **le plus**

Which caterpillar has the most stripes?

Quelle chenille a le plus
de rayures?

mouse **la souris**

a house mouse
une souris
domestique

a computer mouse
une souris
d'ordinateur

mud **la boue**

Sally is covered in mud.
Sally est couverte de boue.

moth **le papillon de nuit**

Moths often
fly toward
lights.

Les
papillons
de nuit volent
souvent vers la lumière.

mouth **la bouche**

Jack is pointing to Polly's mouth.
Jack indique
la bouche
de Polly.

mushroom **le champignon**

Mushrooms grow in fields
and in woods.
Les champignons poussent
dans les
champs
et dans
les bois.

motorcycle **la moto**

This is Steve's new motorcycle.

Voici la moto neuve de Steve.

move (something) déplacer,
(make a move) bouger

The crane is moving the crate.
La grue déplace la caisse.

Don't move! Ne bouge pas!

music **la musique**

Steve, Marco and Molly love music.
Steve, Marco et Molly adorent la
musique.

a b c d e f g h i j k l m n o p q r s t u v w x y z

nail (metal) **le clou,** (fingernail) **l'ongle (m)**

I need some nails to fix the chair.
J'ai besoin de clous pour réparer la chaise.

nail polish
du vernis à ongles

name　　　　**le nom**

Polly is choosing a name for her tiger.
Polly choisit un nom pour son tigre.

narrow　　　　**étroit**

The gap is so narrow that the kitten can't fit through.
Le trou est si étroit que le chaton ne passe pas à travers.

nature　　　　**la nature**

Polly is interested in nature.
Polly s'intéresse à la nature.

naughty　　　　**vilain**

Naughty Pip has stolen Jack's cake.
Le vilain Pip a volé le gâteau de Jack.

near　　　　**près**

The school is near the river.
L'école est près de la rivière.

neck　　　　**le cou**

A giraffe has a very long neck.
La girafe a un cou très long.

necklace　　　　**le collier**

Ruth has a pretty necklace.
Ruth a un joli collier.

need　　　　**avoir besoin**

Sam needs to sleep.
Sam a besoin de dormir.

needle　　　　**l'aiguille (f)**

a sewing needle
une aiguille à coudre

knitting needles
des aiguilles à tricoter

neighbor　　　　**le voisin** **la voisine**

These two people are neighbors.
Ces deux personnes sont voisines.

nest　　　　**le nid**

Birds build nests for their eggs.
Les oiseaux construisent des nids pour leurs œufs.

a b c d e f g h i j k l m n o p q r s t u v w x y z

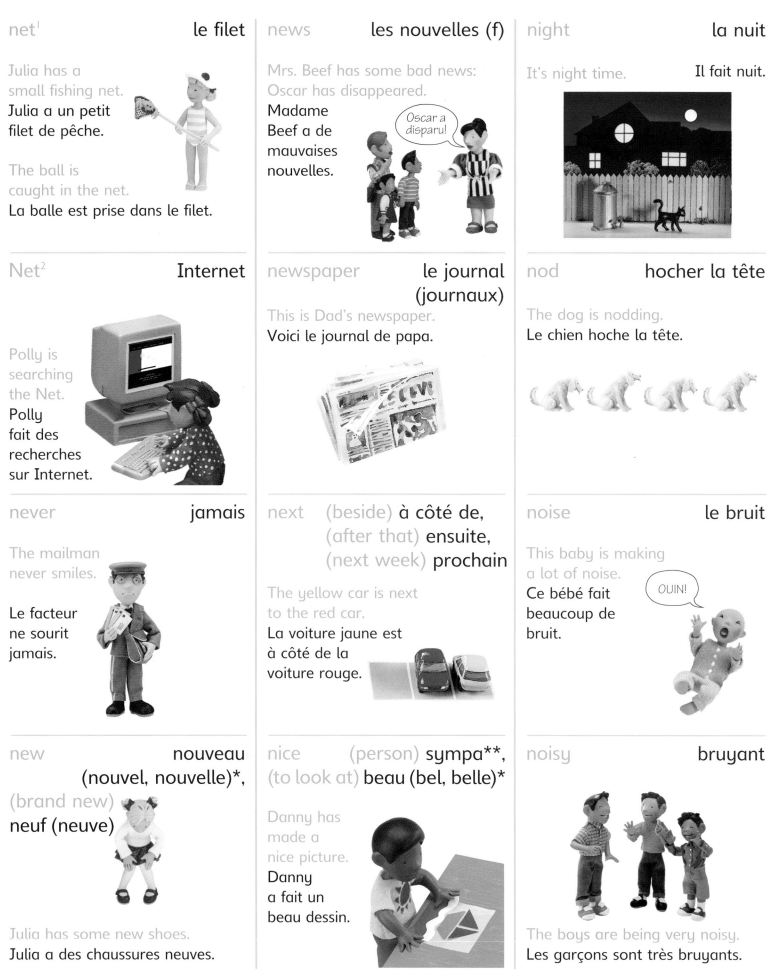

net¹   le filet

Julia has a small fishing net.
Julia a un petit filet de pêche.

The ball is caught in the net.
La balle est prise dans le filet.

Net²   Internet

Polly is searching the Net.
Polly fait des recherches sur Internet.

never   jamais

The mailman never smiles.

Le facteur ne sourit jamais.

new   nouveau (nouvel, nouvelle)*,
(brand new) neuf (neuve)

Julia has some new shoes.
Julia a des chaussures neuves.

news   les nouvelles (f)

Mrs. Beef has some bad news: Oscar has disappeared.
Madame Beef a de mauvaises nouvelles.

Oscar a disparu!

newspaper   le journal (journaux)

This is Dad's newspaper.
Voici le journal de papa.

next   (beside) à côté de, (after that) ensuite, (next week) prochain

The yellow car is next to the red car.
La voiture jaune est à côté de la voiture rouge.

nice   (person) sympa**, (to look at) beau (bel, belle)*

Danny has made a nice picture.
Danny a fait un beau dessin.

night   la nuit

It's night time.   Il fait nuit.

nod   hocher la tête

The dog is nodding.
Le chien hoche la tête.

noise   le bruit

This baby is making a lot of noise.
Ce bébé fait beaucoup de bruit.

OUIN!

noisy   bruyant

The boys are being very noisy.
Les garçons sont très bruyants.

a b c d e f g h i j k l m n o p q r s t u v w x y z

* masculine plural forms: *nouveaux, beaux*
** "sympa" is short for "sympathique", and it is the same for both masculine and feminine.

nose   le nez

Polly is pointing to Jack's nose.
Polly indique le nez de Jack.

note   (message) **le mot,** (music) **la note**

a note for Mr. Dot
un mot pour Monsieur Dot

dentiste 10h30

a low note
une note basse

notebook   le carnet

This is Jack's notebook.
Voici le carnet de Jack.

NOTES

notice   remarquer

Annie hasn't noticed the clown.
Annie n'a pas remarqué le clown.

now   maintenant

The clown is holding a pie...
Le clown tient une tarte...

...now he falls down with his face in it.
...maintenant il tombe, le nez dedans.

number   (figure) **le chiffre,** (quantity) **le nombre,** (street, phone) **le numéro**

(012) 345-6789

My phone number is ten numbers long.
Mon numéro de téléphone a dix chiffres.

nurse   **l'infirmier (m) l'infirmière (f)**

The nurse is pushing Sally in a wheelchair.
L'infirmière pousse Sally dans un fauteuil roulant.

nut   (walnut) **la noix,** (hazelnut) **la noisette,** (almond) **l'amande (f),** (peanut) **la cacahuète**

ocean   l'océan (m)

Oceans are huge seas.

Les océans sont des mers immenses.

o'clock   heure (f), heures

one o'clock in the afternoon
1 heure de l'après-midi

seven o'clock in the evening
7 heures du soir

octopus   la pieuvre

An octopus has eight tentacles.

La pieuvre a huit tentacules.

odd   (number) **impair,** (strange) **curieux (curieuse)**

The blue bunny is jumping on the odd numbers.
Le lapin bleu saute sur les nombres impairs.

1   2   3   4   5

That's odd.   Ça, c'est curieux.

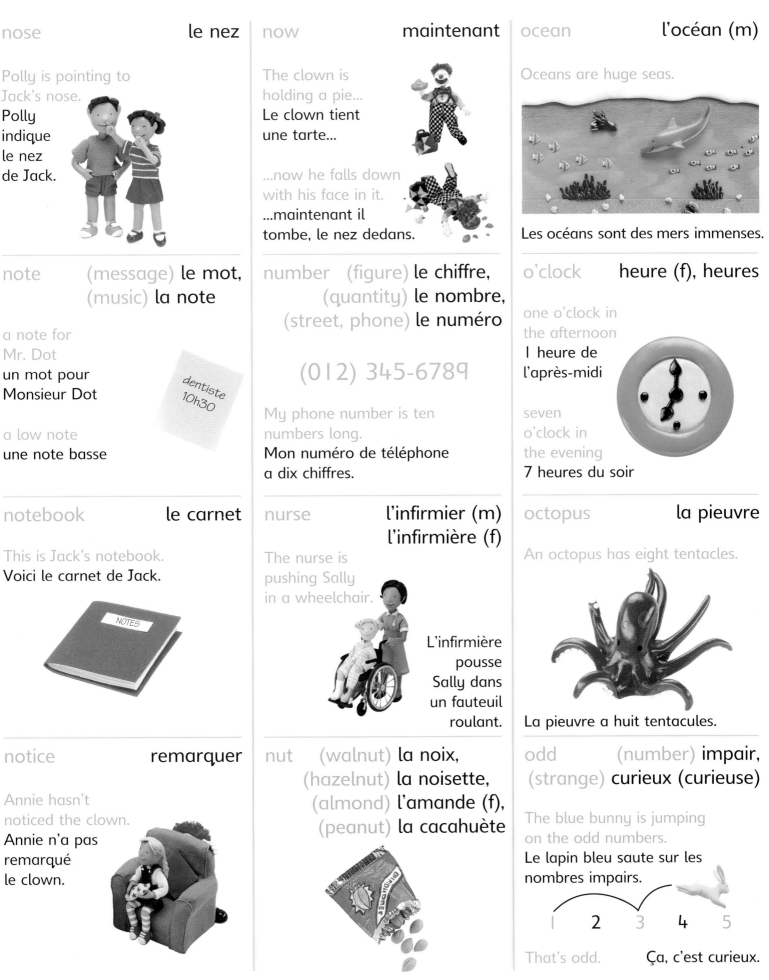

a b c d e f g h i j k l m **n** o p q r s t u v w x y z

often — **souvent**

Mr. Dot and Jack often go and do the shopping.
Monsieur Dot et Jack vont souvent faire les courses.

oil — **l'huile (f)**

Sunflower oil is good for cooking.
L'huile de tournesol est bonne pour la cuisine.

old — **vieux (vieil, vieille)**

an old book
un vieux livre

an old man
un vieil homme

an old shoe
une vieille chaussure

once — **une fois**

They've only been on a balloon ride once.
Ils n'ont fait un voyage en montgolfière qu'une fois.

Once upon a time...
Il était une fois...

onion — **l'oignon (m)**

An onion has a strong taste.
L'oignon a un goût fort.

only — **seulement, ne... que**

Becky only has two strawberries.
Becky a seulement deux fraises
or Becky n'a que deux fraises.

open[1] — **ouvrir**

Mr. Dot is opening the front door.
Monsieur Dot ouvre la porte d'entrée.

Mrs. Dot is opening the box.
Madame Dot ouvre la boîte.

open[2] — **ouvert**

Mrs. Bird's store is open on Saturdays.
Le magasin de Madame Bird est ouvert le samedi.

Ouvert 10h-6h

opposite[1] — **le contraire**

Big is the opposite of small.
Grand est le contraire de petit.

opposite[2] — **en face**

Becky is sitting opposite her teddy bear.
Becky est assise en face de son nounours.

orange — **l'orange (f), (color) orange**

a sweet orange
une orange sucrée

orange paint
de la peinture orange

other — **autre**

Est-ce que tu as d'autres jouets?

Euh, non.

Jenny's asking if Ethan has any other toys.

a b c d e f g h i j k l m n o p q r s t u v w x y z

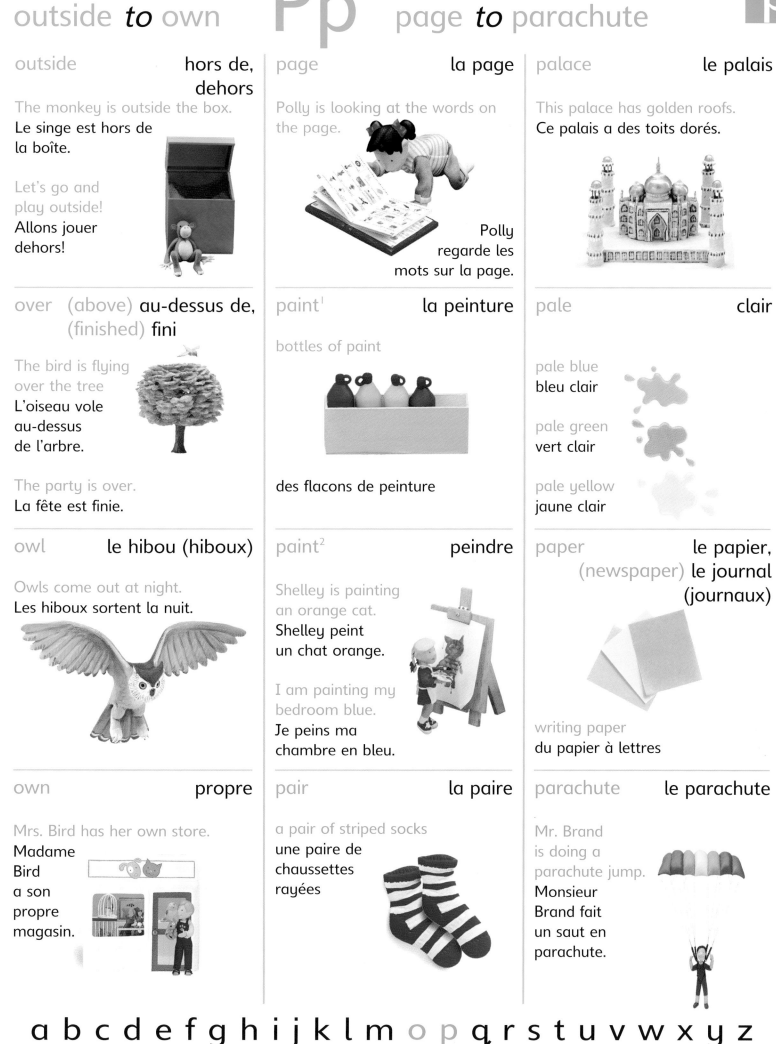

outside — hors de, dehors

The monkey is outside the box.
Le singe est hors de la boîte.

Let's go and play outside!
Allons jouer dehors!

over — (above) au-dessus de, (finished) fini

The bird is flying over the tree
L'oiseau vole au-dessus de l'arbre.

The party is over.
La fête est finie.

owl — le hibou (hiboux)

Owls come out at night.
Les hiboux sortent la nuit.

own — propre

Mrs. Bird has her own store.
Madame Bird a son propre magasin.

page — la page

Polly is looking at the words on the page.
Polly regarde les mots sur la page.

paint¹ — la peinture

bottles of paint
des flacons de peinture

paint² — peindre

Shelley is painting an orange cat.
Shelley peint un chat orange.

I am painting my bedroom blue.
Je peins ma chambre en bleu.

pair — la paire

a pair of striped socks
une paire de chaussettes rayées

palace — le palais

This palace has golden roofs.
Ce palais a des toits dorés.

pale — clair

pale blue
bleu clair

pale green
vert clair

pale yellow
jaune clair

paper — le papier, (newspaper) le journal (journaux)

writing paper
du papier à lettres

parachute — le parachute

Mr. Brand is doing a parachute jump.
Monsieur Brand fait un saut en parachute.

a b c d e f g h i j k l m o p q r s t u v w x y z

parent　　　　le parent

Mr. and Mrs. Dot are Polly and Jack's parents.
Monsieur et Madame Dot sont les parents de Polly et Jack.

park¹　　　　le parc

Let's go and play in the park!
Allons jouer au parc!

park²　　　　garer

Jan parks her car in a parking lot.
Jan gare sa voiture au parking.

parrot　　　　le perroquet

There are some parrots that can talk.
Il y a des perroquets qui parlent.

part　　　　la pièce,
(of a whole) la partie

a spare part
une pièce de rechange

A wheel is part of a car.
Une roue fait partie d'une voiture.

party　　　　la fête

There are lots of guests at Ellie's party.
Il y a beaucoup d'invités à la fête d'Ellie.

pass (go past) passer devant,
(give) passer, (test) réussir

They are passing the bank.
Ils passent devant la banque.

Pass the salt!
Passe-moi le sel!

I passed the exam.
J'ai réussi à l'examen.

past¹　　　　le passé

clothes from the past
des vêtements du temps passé

past²　　　　au-delà de

They run past the stores.
Ils courent au-delà des magasins.

path　　　　le sentier

This path goes to the village.
Ce sentier va au village.

paw　　　　la patte

This is the tiger's paw.
Voici la patte du tigre.

pay　　　　payer

Ethan is paying for his apple.
Ethan paie sa pomme.

a b c d e f g h i j k l m n o **p** q r s t u v w x y z

pea   le petit pois

Peas are green vegetables.
Les petits pois sont des légumes verts.

pear   la poire

a nice, sweet, green pear
une belle poire verte sucrée

penguin   le manchot

Penguins live at the South Pole.
Les manchots vivent au pôle Sud.

peach   la pêche

This peach is delicious.
Cette pêche est délicieuse.

pebble   le galet

There are lots of pebbles by the sea.
Il y a beaucoup de galets au bord de la mer.

people   les gens (m *or* f)

These people are waiting for the concert to start.
Ces gens attendent le début du concert.

peak (mountain) **le sommet**, (cap) **la visière**

There is snow on the peak.
Il y a de la neige au sommet.

a cap with a peak
une casquette à visière

pen   le stylo

This is my nice, new pen.
Voici mon beau stylo neuf.

pepper (spice) **le poivre**, (vegetable) **le poivron**

a pepper mill
un moulin à poivre

green, red and yellow peppers
des poivrons rouges, verts et jaunes

peanut   la cacahuète

a package of salted peanuts
un paquet de cacahuètes salées

pencil   le crayon

I am drawing in pencil.
Je dessine au crayon.

person   la personne

There is only one person here.
Il n'y a qu'une personne ici.

a b c d e f g h i j k l m n o p q r s t u v w x y z

pet l'animal domestique (m)
(animaux domestiques)

some pets

quelques animaux domestiques

phone **le téléphone**

a phone call
un coup de téléphone

or **un coup de fil**

photo **la photo**

Polly is
looking at
some photos.
Polly regarde des photos.

piano **le piano**

Polly has a little, pink piano.
Polly a un petit piano rose.

pick (choose) **choisir,**
(flowers, fruit) **cueillir**

Oliver has
picked an
apple and
a muffin.

Oliver a
choisi une
pomme et
un gâteau.

I'm picking some flowers.
Je cueille des fleurs.

picnic **le pique-nique**

Amy is having a picnic.
**Amy fait un
pique-nique.**

picture **le tableau (tableaux)**

Shelley's painted
a nice picture.
**Shelley a fait
un beau
tableau.**

piece **le morceau (morceaux),**
(part) **la pièce**

a jigsaw
puzzle
with
nine
pieces

**un puzzle
de neuf pièces**

pillow **l'oreiller (m)**

a big, soft pillow
un grand oreiller doux

pilot **le pilote**

Jim wants to
be a pilot.
**Jim veut
être pilote.**

pineapple **l'ananas (m)**

A pineapple is a tropical fruit.
L'ananas est un fruit tropical.

pizza **la pizza**

a vegetarian pizza
une pizza végétarienne

a b c d e f g h i j k l m n o **p** q r s t u v w x y z

place l'endroit (m), le lieu (lieux)

a good place to have lunch
un bon endroit pour déjeuner

plan¹ le plan

a plan of the first floor

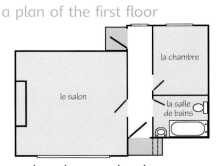

un plan du premier étage

plan² organiser

Mrs. Dot is planning a party.

Madame Dot organise une fête.

plane l'avion (m)

This plane is landing.
Cet avion atterrit.

planet la planète

a planet with rings around it
une planète entourée d'anneaux

plant la plante

This is a house plant.
Voici une plante d'intérieur.

plate l'assiette (f)

My plate is clean.
Mon assiette est propre.

play jouer

The children are playing outside.
Les enfants jouent dehors.

Neil is playing soccer.
Neil joue au foot.

Polly is playing the piano.
Polly joue du piano.

playground l'aire de jeux (f), (school) la cour de récréation

the playground in the park

l'aire de jeux du parc

please s'il te plaît s'il vous plaît*

Becky is asking if she can please have some more strawberries.

Je peux avoir encore des fraises s'il te plaît?

plum la prune

a nice, ripe plum
une belle prune mûre

pocket la poche

Renata is putting her hands in her pockets.
Renata met les mains dans ses poches.

a b c d e f g h i j k l m n o p q r s t u v w x y z

* For the difference between *tu* and *vous*, see page 4.

poem — le poème

Shelley has written a poem about her cat.
Shelley a écrit un poème sur son chat.

Mon chat

Mon chat est tout petit
Il ronronne dans son lit
Il sait miauler
Pour réclamer du lait
Mon chat est tout petit
Quand il vient dans mon lit
On n'entend aucun bruit.

point¹ (sharp) la pointe, (score) le point

the pencil point
la pointe du crayon

We're playing a game, and I have forty points.
Nous faisons un jeu, et j'ai quarante points.

point² — indiquer

Polly is pointing to Jack's nose.
Polly indique le nez de Jack.

police — la police

Brian works for the police.
Brian travaille dans la police.

police car — la voiture de police

There is no one in the police car.
Il n'y a personne dans la voiture de police.

pond — l'étang (m)

There is a duck on the pond.
Il y a un canard sur l'étang.

pony — le poney

a small pony
un petit poney

pool — la piscine

There's a children's pool in the park.
Il y a une piscine pour enfants dans le parc.

poor — pauvre

rich people and poor people
les riches et les pauvres

Poor Ross, his tummy hurts.
Le pauvre Ross, il a mal au ventre.

potato — la pomme de terre

Potatoes grow underground.
Les pommes de terre poussent sous terre.

present — le cadeau (cadeaux)

This is a surprise present for Polly.
Voici un cadeau surprise pour Polly.

press — appuyer

Danny is pressing down the blue paper.
Danny appuie sur le papier bleu.

a b c d e f g h i j k l m n o p q r s t u v w x y z

pretend **faire semblant**

Nicholas is pretending to sleep.

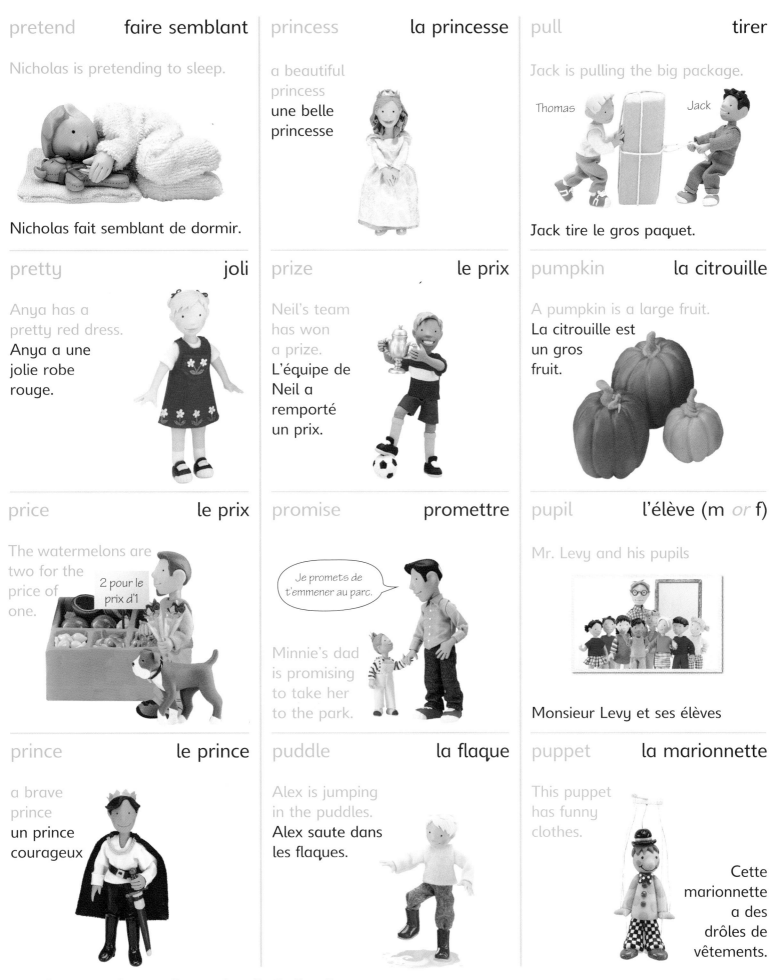

Nicholas fait semblant de dormir.

pretty **joli**

Anya has a
pretty red dress.
Anya a une
jolie robe
rouge.

price **le prix**

The watermelons are
two for the
price of
one.

2 pour le
prix d'1

prince **le prince**

a brave
prince
un prince
courageux

princess **la princesse**

a beautiful
princess
une belle
princesse

prize **le prix**

Neil's team
has won
a prize.
L'équipe de
Neil a
remporté
un prix.

promise **promettre**

Je promets de
t'emmener au parc.

Minnie's dad
is promising
to take her
to the park.

puddle **la flaque**

Alex is jumping
in the puddles.
Alex saute dans
les flaques.

pull **tirer**

Jack is pulling the big package.

Thomas   Jack

Jack tire le gros paquet.

pumpkin **la citrouille**

A pumpkin is a large fruit.
La citrouille est
un gros
fruit.

pupil **l'élève (m *or* f)**

Mr. Levy and his pupils

Monsieur Levy et ses élèves

puppet **la marionnette**

This puppet
has funny
clothes.

Cette
marionnette
a des
drôles de
vêtements.

a b c d e f g h i j k l m n o p q r s t u v w x y z

puppy le chiot

The yellow dog has a very sweet puppy.

Le chien jaune a un chiot très mignon.

push pousser

Thomas is pushing the big package.

Thomas

Jack

Thomas pousse le gros paquet.

put mettre, (put down) poser

Oliver is putting the bottle of paint on the table.

Oliver pose le flacon de peinture sur la table.

puzzle le casse-tête

This isn't a difficult puzzle.

Ce n'est pas un casse-tête difficile.

quack cancaner

A duck quacks.

Un canard cancane.

Coin! Coin!

quarter le quart

a quarter of the cake

le quart du gâteau

quarter past three

3 heures et quart

queen la reine

Joy is dressed up as a queen.

Joy est déguisée en reine.

question la question

Polly is asking a question: what's the clown's name?

Comment tu t'appelles?

Polly pose une question.

quick vite

Grace is very quick on her skateboard.

Grace va très vite sur sa planche à roulettes.

quiet doux (douce), (silent) silencieux (silencieuse)

Anna is so quiet that Milo doesn't hear her.

Anna est si silencieuse que Milo ne l'entend pas.

quite (fairly) assez, (completely) tout à fait

I'm quite tired.

Je suis assez fatigué.

Mr. Bun isn't quite ready.

Monsieur Bun n'est pas tout à fait prêt.

quiz le concours

This is a quiz about animals.

Voici un concours sur les animaux.

Les animaux
1) Quel est le plus grand animal du monde?
2) Quel genre d'animal est le toucan?
3) Où irais-tu dans le monde pour voir des autruches et des guépards?

a b c d e f g h i j k l m n o **p** q r s t u v w x y z

62

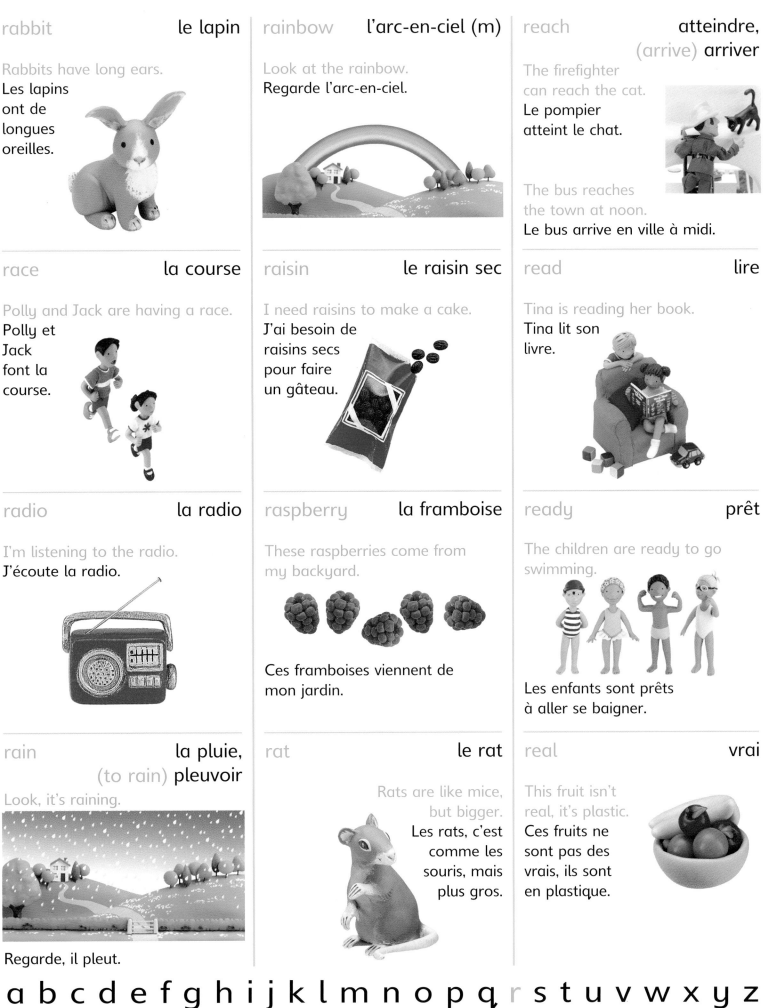

rabbit   le lapin

Rabbits have long ears.
Les lapins ont de longues oreilles.

rainbow   l'arc-en-ciel (m)

Look at the rainbow.
Regarde l'arc-en-ciel.

reach   atteindre, (arrive) arriver

The firefighter can reach the cat.
Le pompier atteint le chat.

The bus reaches the town at noon.
Le bus arrive en ville à midi.

race   la course

Polly and Jack are having a race.
Polly et Jack font la course.

raisin   le raisin sec

I need raisins to make a cake.
J'ai besoin de raisins secs pour faire un gâteau.

read   lire

Tina is reading her book.
Tina lit son livre.

radio   la radio

I'm listening to the radio.
J'écoute la radio.

raspberry   la framboise

These raspberries come from my backyard.
Ces framboises viennent de mon jardin.

ready   prêt

The children are ready to go swimming.
Les enfants sont prêts à aller se baigner.

rain   la pluie, (to rain) pleuvoir

Look, it's raining.
Regarde, il pleut.

rat   le rat

Rats are like mice, but bigger.
Les rats, c'est comme les souris, mais plus gros.

real   vrai

This fruit isn't real, it's plastic.
Ces fruits ne sont pas des vrais, ils sont en plastique.

a b c d e f g h i j k l m n o p q r s t u v w x y z

recorder — **la flûte à bec**

I'm learning to play the recorder at school.

J'apprends à jouer de la flûte à bec à l'école.

refrigerator — **le réfrigérateur** *or* **le frigo**

The refrigerator is full of good things to eat.

Le frigo est plein de bonnes choses à manger.

remember — **se rappeler, se souvenir**

Fiona can remember the date of her friend's birthday.

Ton anniversaire, c'est le 26 mai.

Fiona se souvient de la date d'anniversaire de son amie.

reply — **répondre**

Tu veux aller au parc?

Oui, s'il te plaît.

Minnie is replying to her dad.

Minnie répond à son papa.

rescue — **sauver**

Mr. Sparks has rescued the cat.

Monsieur Sparks a sauvé le chat.

rhinoceros — **le rhinocéros** *or* rhino

Rhinos live in hot countries.

Les rhinocéros vivent dans les pays chauds.

ribbon — **le ruban**

Becky has green ribbons.

Becky a des rubans verts.

rice — **le riz**

I prefer rice over pasta.

Je préfère le riz aux pâtes.

rich — **riche**

Natalie is a rich popstar.

Natalie est une star riche.

ride (horse) **monter à cheval,** (bicycle) **faire du vélo**

Martin can ride.

Martin sait monter à cheval.

right (not left) **droite,** (not wrong) **bon (bonne)**

Greta has put the puppet on her right hand.

Greta a mis la marionnette à sa main droite.

That's the right answer.

C'est la bonne réponse.

ring¹ (jewelry) **la bague,** (shape) **l'anneau (m) (anneaux)**

a ring with a red stone

une bague avec une pierre rouge

the rings of Saturn

les anneaux de Saturne

a b c d e f g h i j k l m n o p q **r** s t u v w x y z

ring² — sonner

The phone's ringing.
Le téléphone
sonne.

drring!

ripe — mûr

The melon, the avocado and the watermelon are all ripe.

Le melon, l'avocat et la pastèque sont tous mûrs.

river — la rivière, (big river) le fleuve

The houses are near the river.
Les maisons sont près du fleuve.

road — la route

The road goes to the town center.
La route va au centre-ville.

robot — le robot

This robot is a toy.
Ce robot est
un jouet.

rock — (stone) le rocher, (music) le rock

There are rocks
on the beach.
Il y a des rochers
à la plage.

Steve likes
playing rock.
Steve aime
jouer du rock.

rocket — la fusée

This rocket is only a toy.
Cette fusée n'est qu'un jouet.

roof — le toit

The roof of this building is blue.
Le toit de ce
bâtiment
est
bleu.

room — (in house) la pièce, (space) la place

On this plan,
there are six rooms.
Sur ce plan, il y a
six pièces.

Is there some
room for me?
Est-ce qu'il y a de
la place pour moi?

rope — la corde

Jack needs a rope to
pull the big package.

Jack a besoin d'une
corde pour tirer le
gros paquet.

rose — la rose

Roses are my favorite flowers.
Les roses sont mes fleurs
préférées.

round — rond

In general,
drums are
round.

En général,
les tambours
sont ronds.

a b c d e f g h i j k l m n o p q r s t u v w x y z

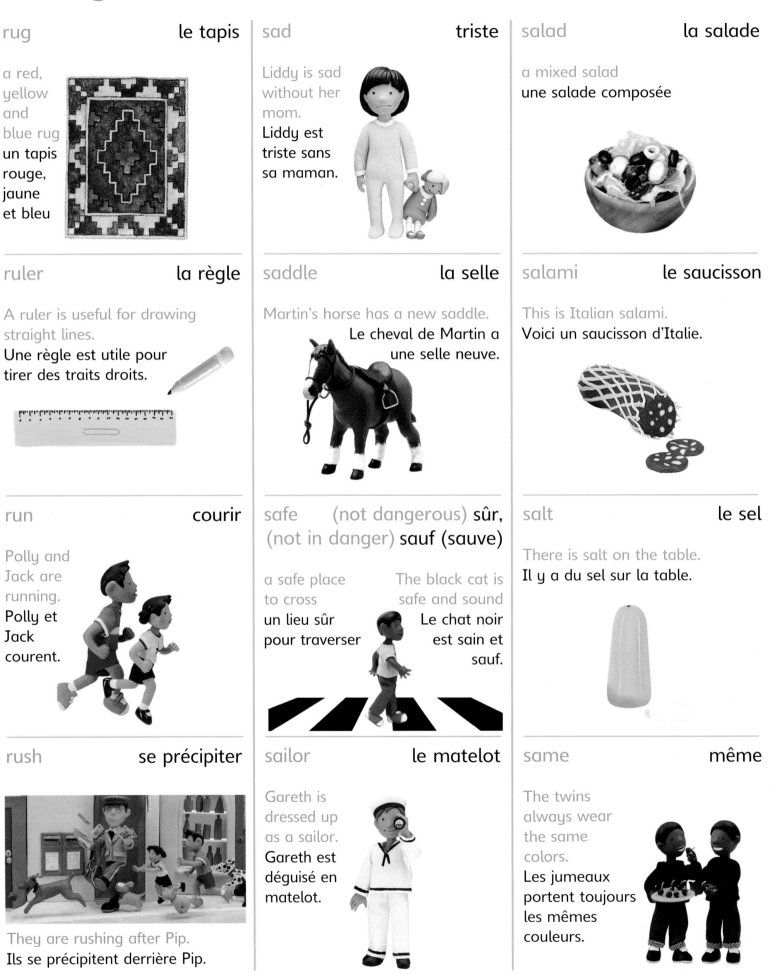

rug — le tapis

a red, yellow and blue rug
un tapis rouge, jaune et bleu

ruler — la règle

A ruler is useful for drawing straight lines.
Une règle est utile pour tirer des traits droits.

run — courir

Polly and Jack are running.
Polly et Jack courent.

rush — se précipiter

They are rushing after Pip.
Ils se précipitent derrière Pip.

sad — triste

Liddy is sad without her mom.
Liddy est triste sans sa maman.

saddle — la selle

Martin's horse has a new saddle.
Le cheval de Martin a une selle neuve.

safe (not dangerous) **sûr,** (not in danger) **sauf (sauve)**

a safe place to cross
un lieu sûr pour traverser

The black cat is safe and sound
Le chat noir est sain et sauf.

sailor — le matelot

Gareth is dressed up as a sailor.
Gareth est déguisé en matelot.

salad — la salade

a mixed salad
une salade composée

salami — le saucisson

This is Italian salami.
Voici un saucisson d'Italie.

salt — le sel

There is salt on the table.
Il y a du sel sur la table.

same — même

The twins always wear the same colors.
Les jumeaux portent toujours les mêmes couleurs.

a b c d e f g h i j k l m n o p q r s t u v w x y z

66

sand *to* scooter

sand le sable

The children are playing in the sand.
Les enfants jouent dans le sable.

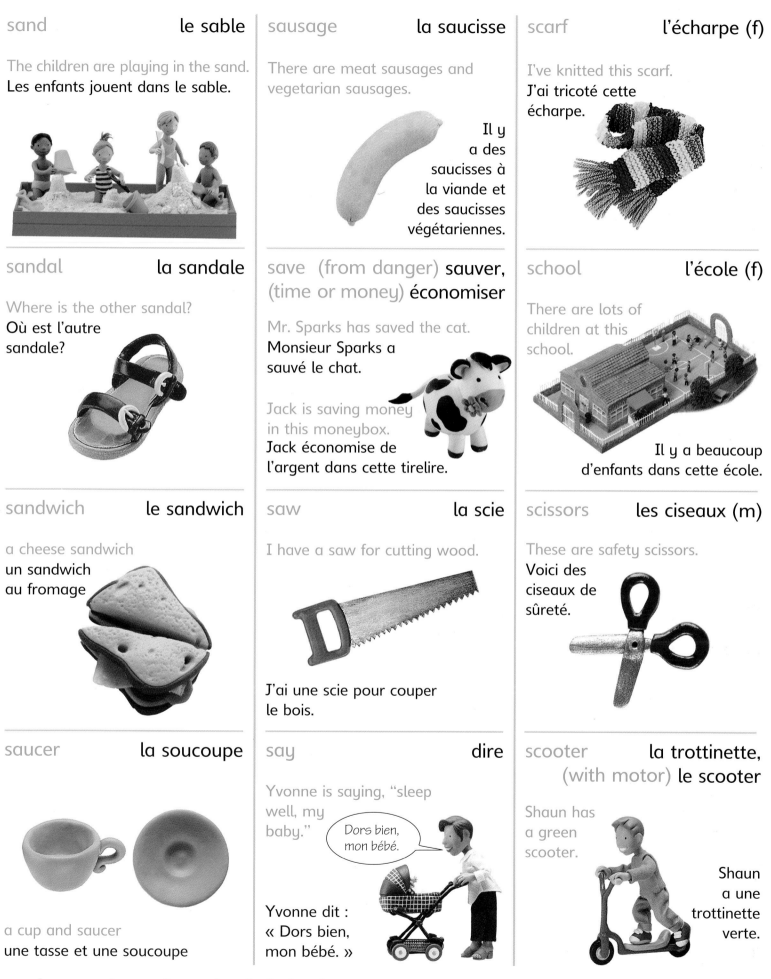

sandal la sandale

Where is the other sandal?
Où est l'autre sandale?

sandwich le sandwich

a cheese sandwich
un sandwich au fromage

saucer la soucoupe

a cup and saucer
une tasse et une soucoupe

sausage la saucisse

There are meat sausages and vegetarian sausages.
Il y a des saucisses à la viande et des saucisses végétariennes.

save (from danger) **sauver,**
(time or money) **économiser**

Mr. Sparks has saved the cat.
Monsieur Sparks a sauvé le chat.

Jack is saving money in this moneybox.
Jack économise de l'argent dans cette tirelire.

saw la scie

I have a saw for cutting wood.
J'ai une scie pour couper le bois.

say dire

Yvonne is saying, "sleep well, my baby."
Dors bien, mon bébé.
Yvonne dit :
« Dors bien, mon bébé. »

scarf l'écharpe (f)

I've knitted this scarf.
J'ai tricoté cette écharpe.

school l'école (f)

There are lots of children at this school.
Il y a beaucoup d'enfants dans cette école.

scissors les ciseaux (m)

These are safety scissors.
Voici des ciseaux de sûreté.

scooter la trottinette,
(with motor) **le scooter**

Shaun has a green scooter.
Shaun a une trottinette verte.

a b c d e f g h i j k l m n o p q r s t u v w x y z

sea	**la mer**

The sea is calm today.

La mer est calme aujourd'hui.

secret	**le secret**

Amy is telling Anna a secret.
Amy raconte un secret à Anna.

sentence	**la phrase**

This is a complete sentence.

My dad likes apples.
Mon papa aime les pommes.

Voici une phrase complète.

seal	**le phoque**

Seals live by the sea.
Les phoques vivent au bord de la mer.

see	**voir**

Annie can't see the clown.
Annie ne voit pas le clown.

I'm going to see my grandparents.
Je vais voir mes grands-parents.

sew	**coudre**

Robert is sewing his shirt.
Robert coud sa chemise.

search	**chercher**

They are searching for their friend.
Ils cherchent leur ami.

sell	**vendre**

Mrs. Hussain is selling Ethan an apple.
Madame Hussain vend une pomme à Ethan.

shadow	**l'ombre (f)**

Look at Robert's shadow!
Regarde l'ombre de Robert!

seat	(chair) **le siège,** (place to sit) **la place**

There are three seats free.

Il y a trois places libres.

send	**envoyer**

Jack is sending a letter to his friend.
Jack envoie une lettre à son ami.

shake	**secouer**

Anton likes shaking his rattle.
Anton aime secouer son hochet.

a b c d e f g h i j k l m n o p q r **s** t u v w x y z

shallow   **peu profond**

The children's pool
is very shallow.

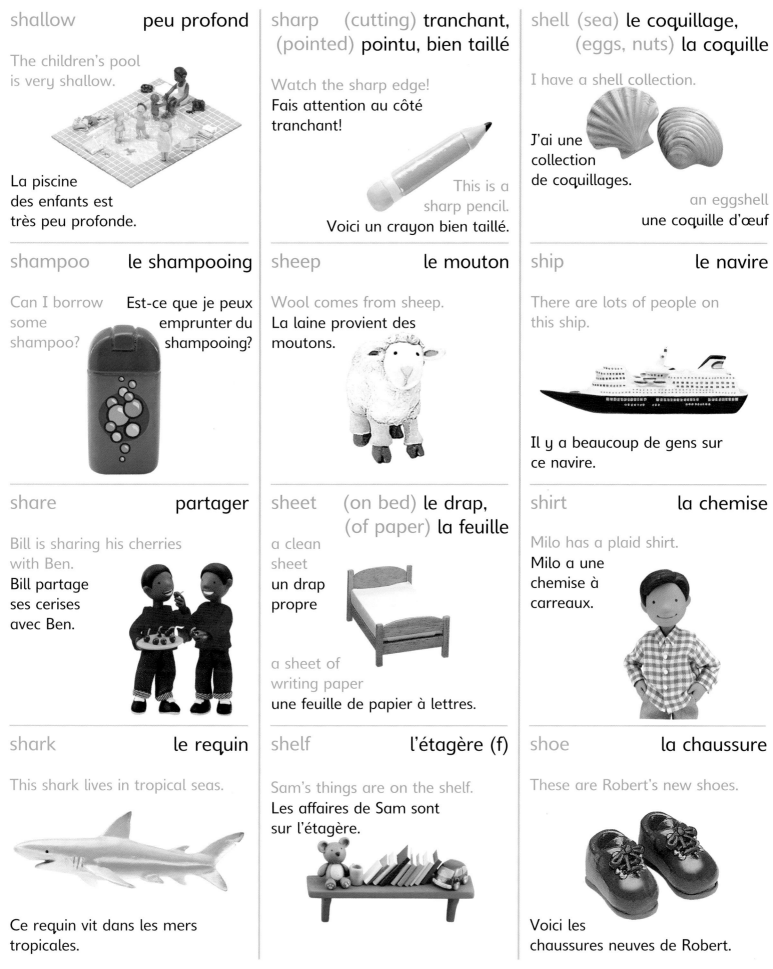

La piscine
des enfants est
très peu profonde.

shampoo   **le shampooing**

Can I borrow   Est-ce que je peux
some   emprunter du
shampoo?   shampooing?

share   **partager**

Bill is sharing his cherries
with Ben.

**Bill partage
ses cerises
avec Ben.**

shark   **le requin**

This shark lives in tropical seas.

Ce requin vit dans les mers
tropicales.

sharp   (cutting) **tranchant,**
(pointed) **pointu, bien taillé**

Watch the sharp edge!
**Fais attention au côté
tranchant!**

This is a
sharp pencil.
Voici un crayon bien taillé.

sheep   **le mouton**

Wool comes from sheep.
**La laine provient des
moutons.**

sheet   (on bed) **le drap,**
(of paper) **la feuille**

a clean
sheet
**un drap
propre**

a sheet of
writing paper
une feuille de papier à lettres.

shelf   **l'étagère (f)**

Sam's things are on the shelf.
**Les affaires de Sam sont
sur l'étagère.**

shell (sea) **le coquillage,**
(eggs, nuts) **la coquille**

I have a shell collection.

J'ai une
collection
de coquillages.

an eggshell
une coquille d'œuf

ship   **le navire**

There are lots of people on
this ship.

Il y a beaucoup de gens sur
ce navire.

shirt   **la chemise**

Milo has a plaid shirt.
**Milo a une
chemise à
carreaux.**

shoe   **la chaussure**

These are Robert's new shoes.

Voici les
chaussures neuves de Robert.

a b c d e f g h i j k l m n o p q r s t u v w x y z

short **court**

Maisie has
short hair.
Maisie a
les cheveux
courts.

shorts **le short**

brightly colored shorts

un short aux couleurs vives

shoulder **l'épaule (f)**

This is Jack's shoulder.
Voici l'épaule
de Jack.

shout **hurler**

ARRÊTE,
PIP!

Jack is shouting,
"Stop, Pip!"
Jack hurle : « Arrête, Pip ! »

show **montrer**

Jack is showing
Thomas his hands.
Jack montre
ses mains à
Thomas.

Show me
what to do.
Montre-moi quoi faire.

shower **(to wash) la douche,**
(rain) l'averse (f)

Robert is
taking a
shower.
Robert
prend sa
douche.

sun and
showers
soleil et averses

shrink **rétrécir**

Wool clothes
often shrink
in hot water.
Les vêtements
de laine
rétrécissent
souvent à
l'eau chaude.

shut **fermer**

Danny is shutting
the door.
Danny ferme
la porte.

side **(edge, face) le côté,**
(team) l'équipe (f)

I write on both sides of the paper.
J'écris des deux côtés
du papier.

He's on the
other side.
Il est dans
l'équipe opposée.

sign¹ **(symbol) le symbole,**
(road) le panneau (panneaux)

@ is the sign for "at".
@ est le symbole
pour "à".

This sign means
"no buses".
Ce panneau veut dire
"interdit aux bus".

sign² **signer**

The paper says "Sign please".

Signez SVP

since **depuis**

VERS CENTRE-VILLE
22

They've been waiting since noon.
Ils attendent depuis midi.

a b c d e f g h i j k l m n o p q r **s** t u v w x y z

sing   chanter

Molly can sing very well.
Molly chante très bien.

sink¹   (kitchen) l'évier (m),
        (bathroom) le lavabo

The sink is empty.
Le lavabo est vide.

sink²   couler

Billy's boat is sinking.
Le bateau de Billy coule.

sit   (sit down) s'asseoir,
         (be sitting) être assis

Sally is sitting on a blue stool.
Sally est assise sur un tabouret bleu.

size   la taille

This T-shirt is the right size for Zoe.
Ce t-shirt est à la bonne taille pour Zoe.

skate   faire du patin

Gemma is ice skating.
Gemma fait du patin à glace.

ski   faire du ski

Eric skis every day in winter.
Eric fait du ski tous les jours en hiver.

skin   la peau (peaux)

Don't eat the banana skin!
Ne mange pas la peau de banane!

Babies have smooth skin.
Les bébés ont la peau lisse.

skirt   la jupe

This skirt has four red buttons.
Cette jupe a quatre boutons rouges.

sky   le ciel (cieux)

There's a plane in the sky.
Il y a un avion dans le ciel.

sleep   dormir

Shhh! Adam is sleeping.
Chut! Adam dort.

sleeve   la manche

Robert has a yellow top with blue sleeves.
Robert a un haut jaune aux manches bleues.

a b c d e f g h i j k l m n o p q r s t u v w x y z

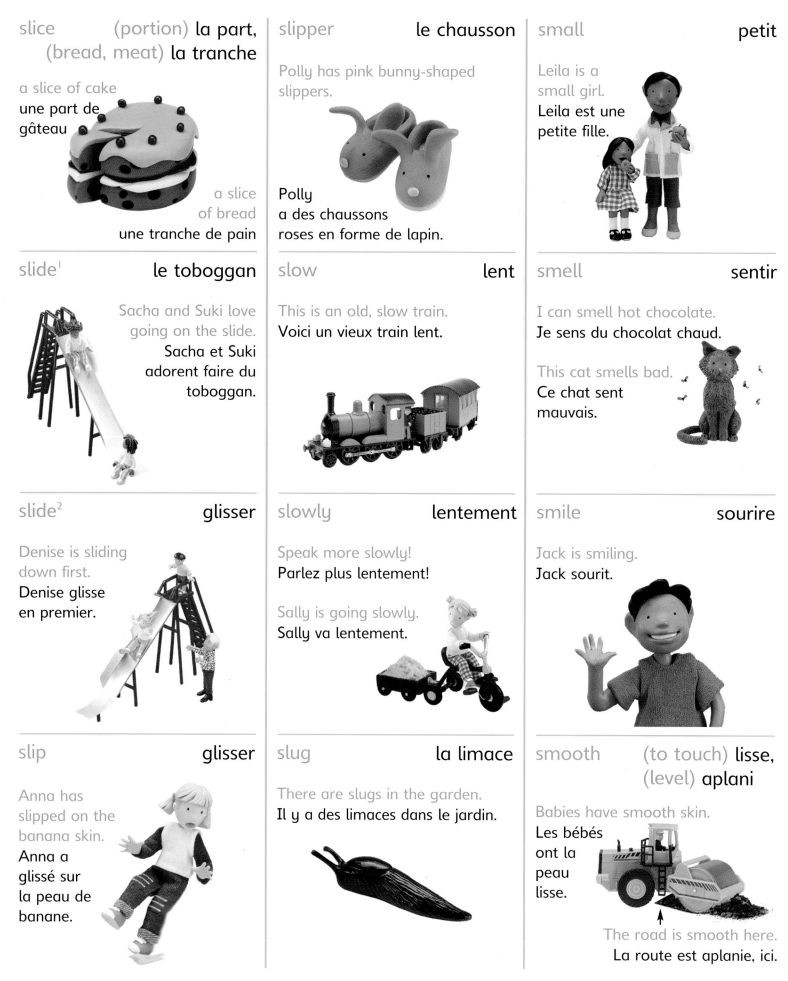

slice (portion) **la part,** (bread, meat) **la tranche**

a slice of cake
une part de gâteau

a slice of bread
une tranche de pain

slipper **le chausson**

Polly has pink bunny-shaped slippers.

Polly a des chaussons roses en forme de lapin.

small **petit**

Leila is a small girl.
Leila est une petite fille.

slide¹ **le toboggan**

Sacha and Suki love going on the slide.
Sacha et Suki adorent faire du toboggan.

slow **lent**

This is an old, slow train.
Voici un vieux train lent.

smell **sentir**

I can smell hot chocolate.
Je sens du chocolat chaud.

This cat smells bad.
Ce chat sent mauvais.

slide² **glisser**

Denise is sliding down first.
Denise glisse en premier.

slowly **lentement**

Speak more slowly!
Parlez plus lentement!

Sally is going slowly.
Sally va lentement.

smile **sourire**

Jack is smiling.
Jack sourit.

slip **glisser**

Anna has slipped on the banana skin.
Anna a glissé sur la peau de banane.

slug **la limace**

There are slugs in the garden.
Il y a des limaces dans le jardin.

smooth (to touch) **lisse,** (level) **aplani**

Babies have smooth skin.
Les bébés ont la peau lisse.

The road is smooth here.
La route est aplanie, ici.

a b c d e f g h i j k l m n o p q r **s** t u v w x y z

snail l'escargot (m)

A snail is like a slug with a shell.
L'escargot, c'est comme une limace avec une coquille.

snake le serpent

There's a snake in the tree.
Il y a un serpent dans l'arbre.

snow la neige,
(to snow) neiger

They're playing in the snow.
Ils jouent dans la neige.

soap le savon

My soap is pink.
Mon savon est rose.

soccer le foot

Neil plays soccer every Saturday.
Neil joue au foot tous les samedis.

sock la chaussette

Luke has striped socks.
Luke a des chaussettes à rayures.

sofa le canapé

Alexa is reading on the sofa.
Alexa lit sur le canapé.

soft doux (douce)

The white kitten has soft fur.
Le chaton blanc a des poils doux.

soil la terre

It's good soil for my plant.
C'est de la bonne terre pour ma plante.

soldier le soldat

Tony is dressed up as a soldier.
Tony est déguisé en soldat.

song la chanson

boom ba ba, boom ba ba

Natalie is singing a song.
Natalie chante une chanson.

soon bientôt

It will soon be two o'clock.

Il sera bientôt 2 heures.

a b c d e f g h i j k l m n o p q r s t u v w x y z

sort — la sorte, le genre, l'espèce (f)

different sorts of food
différentes sortes d'aliments

sound — le bruit

Salut!

That funny sound is the parrot.
Ce drôle de bruit, c'est le perroquet.

soup — la soupe

a can of vegetable soup
une boîte de soupe aux légumes

space — (room) la place, (stars) l'espace (m)

There are two free spaces.
Il y a deux places libres.

Astronauts go into space.
Les astronautes vont dans l'espace.

spacecraft — le vaisseau spatial (vaisseaux spatiaux)

A rocket is a spacecraft.
Une fusée, c'est un vaisseau spatial.

speak — parler

Mrs. Rose is speaking to her friend.

Bonjour! Bonjour!

Madame Rose parle avec son amie.

special — spécial*

something special to eat
quelque chose de spécial à manger

Electricians need special tools
Les électriciens ont besoin d'outils spéciaux.

spell¹ — le sort

The witch is casting a spell.
La sorcière jette un sort.

spell² — épeler

Oliver can spell his first name
Oliver sait épeler son prénom.

OLIVER

spend — dépenser

Danny has some money to spend.
Danny a de l'argent à dépenser.

spider — l'araignée (f)

Maddy hates spiders, but I don't mind them.

Maddy déteste les araignées, mais elles ne me dérangent pas.

spill — renverser

The cat has spilled some mustard.

Le chat a renversé de la moutarde.

a b c d e f g h i j k l m n o p q r s t u v w x y z

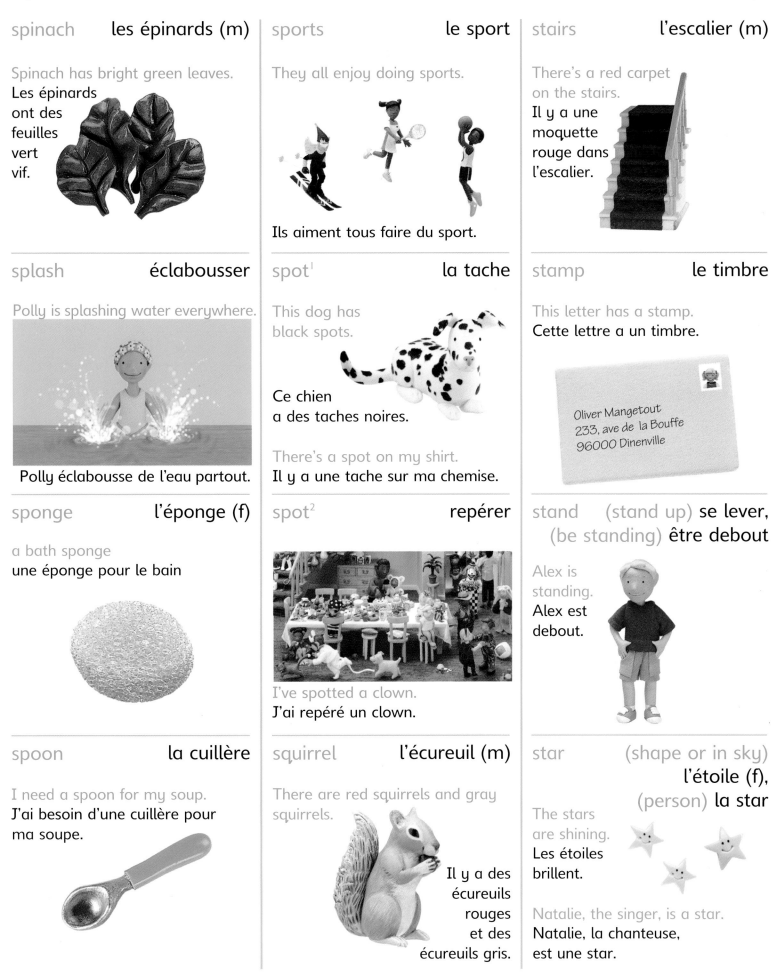

spinach les épinards (m)

Spinach has bright green leaves.
Les épinards
ont des
feuilles
vert
vif.

sports le sport

They all enjoy doing sports.

Ils aiment tous faire du sport.

stairs l'escalier (m)

There's a red carpet
on the stairs.
Il y a une
moquette
rouge dans
l'escalier.

splash éclabousser

Polly is splashing water everywhere.

Polly éclabousse de l'eau partout.

spot¹ la tache

This dog has
black spots.

Ce chien
a des taches noires.

There's a spot on my shirt.
Il y a une tache sur ma chemise.

stamp le timbre

This letter has a stamp.
Cette lettre a un timbre.

Oliver Mangetout
233, ave de la Bouffe
96000 Dinenville

sponge l'éponge (f)

a bath sponge
une éponge pour le bain

spot² repérer

I've spotted a clown.
J'ai repéré un clown.

stand (stand up) se lever,
(be standing) être debout

Alex is
standing.
Alex est
debout.

spoon la cuillère

I need a spoon for my soup.
J'ai besoin d'une cuillère pour
ma soupe.

squirrel l'écureuil (m)

There are red squirrels and gray
squirrels.

Il y a des
écureuils
rouges
et des
écureuils gris.

star (shape or in sky)
l'étoile (f),
(person) la star

The stars
are shining.
Les étoiles
brillent.

Natalie, the singer, is a star.
Natalie, la chanteuse,
est une star.

a b c d e f g h i j k l m n o p q r **s** t u v w x y z

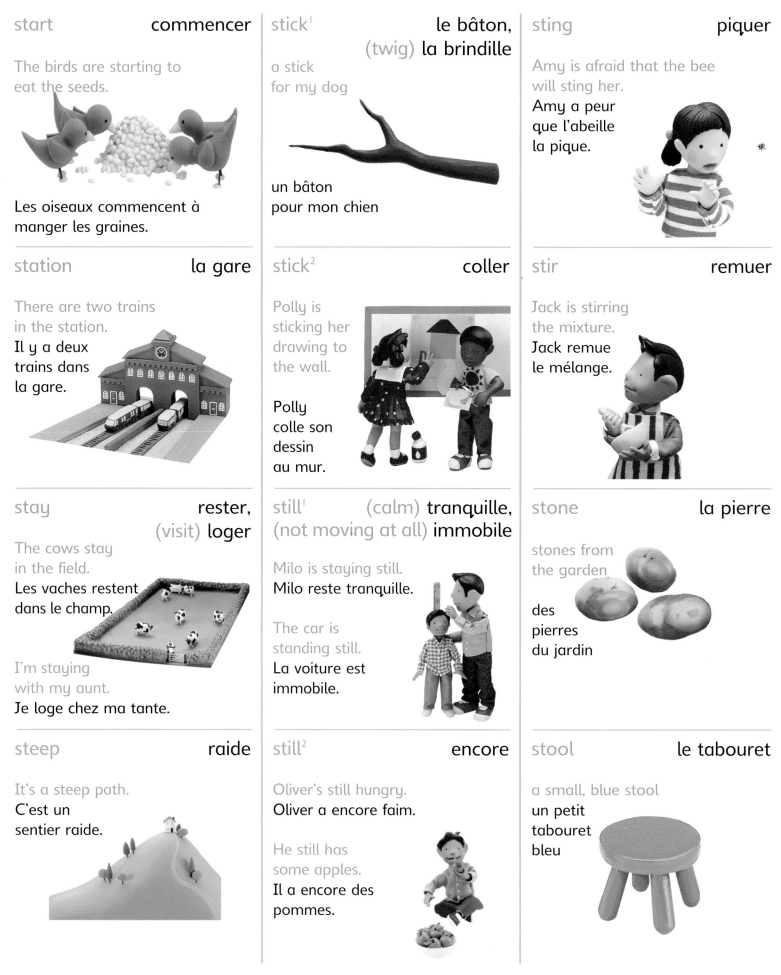

start — **commencer**

The birds are starting to eat the seeds.

Les oiseaux commencent à manger les graines.

station — **la gare**

There are two trains in the station.

Il y a deux trains dans la gare.

stay — **rester,** (visit) **loger**

The cows stay in the field.

Les vaches restent dans le champ.

I'm staying with my aunt.

Je loge chez ma tante.

steep — **raide**

It's a steep path.

C'est un sentier raide.

stick¹ — **le bâton,** (twig) **la brindille**

a stick for my dog

un bâton pour mon chien

stick² — **coller**

Polly is sticking her drawing to the wall.

Polly colle son dessin au mur.

still¹ — (calm) **tranquille,** (not moving at all) **immobile**

Milo is staying still.

Milo reste tranquille.

The car is standing still.

La voiture est immobile.

still² — **encore**

Oliver's still hungry.

Oliver a encore faim.

He still has some apples.

Il a encore des pommes.

sting — **piquer**

Amy is afraid that the bee will sting her.

Amy a peur que l'abeille la pique.

stir — **remuer**

Jack is stirring the mixture.

Jack remue le mélange.

stone — **la pierre**

stones from the garden

des pierres du jardin

stool — **le tabouret**

a small, blue stool

un petit tabouret bleu

a b c d e f g h i j k l m n o p q r s t u v w x y z

stop *to* sugar

stop — arrêter, (yourself) s'arrêter

Jan is stopping at the gate.
Jan s'arrête à la barrière.

The police are stopping the cars.
La police arrête les voitures.

storm — la tempête

a storm at sea
une tempête en mer

story — l'histoire (f)

Polly is writing a story.
Polly écrit une histoire.

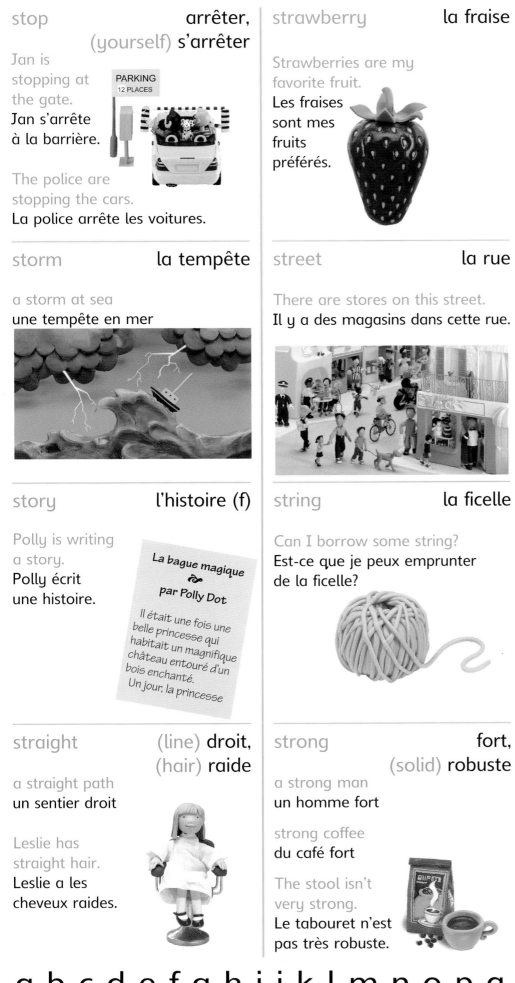

La bague magique
par Polly Dot

Il était une fois une belle princesse qui habitait un magnifique château entouré d'un bois enchanté.
Un jour, la princesse

straight — (line) droit, (hair) raide

a straight path
un sentier droit

Leslie has straight hair.
Leslie a les cheveux raides.

strawberry — la fraise

Strawberries are my favorite fruit.
Les fraises sont mes fruits préférés.

street — la rue

There are stores on this street.
Il y a des magasins dans cette rue.

string — la ficelle

Can I borrow some string?
Est-ce que je peux emprunter de la ficelle?

strong — fort, (solid) robuste

a strong man
un homme fort

strong coffee
du café fort

The stool isn't very strong.
Le tabouret n'est pas très robuste.

study¹ — le bureau (bureaux)

Mom's study   le bureau de maman

study² — étudier

Sara is studying the Romans.
Sara étudie les Romains.

suddenly — tout à coup

Suddenly Asha drops the vase.
Tout à coup, Asha laisse tomber le vase.

sugar — le sucre

I need sugar to make a cake.
J'ai besoin de sucre pour faire un gâteau.

a b c d e f g h i j k l m n o p q r **s** t u v w x y z

suitcase   **la valise**

This is Mr. Brand's suitcase.
Voici la valise de monsieur Brand.

sunglasses   **les lunettes (f) de soleil**

Polly has sunglasses
with blue flowers on them.

**Polly a des lunettes de soleil
avec des fleurs bleues dessus.**

swan   **le cygne**

There's a swan on the river.

Il y a un cygne sur la rivière.

sum   **le calcul**

I can do these sums.
Je sais faire ces calculs.

$$8 + 2 =$$
$$4 - 2 =$$
$$10 \times 4 =$$

supermarket   **le supermarché**

Dad is at the
supermarket.

**Papa
est au
super-
marché.**

sweep   **balayer**

Anna is sweeping
the kitchen.
**Anna balaie
la cuisine.**

sun   **le soleil**

The sun is shining today.
Le soleil brille aujourd'hui.

sure   **sûr**

Dad is sure they've
bought everything.
**Papa est sûr qu'ils
ont tout acheté.**

sweet   **(taste) sucré
(cute) mignon (mignonne)**

The cake
is very sweet.
**Le gâteau est
très sucré.**

This kitten is very sweet.
Ce chaton est très mignon.

sunflower   **le tournesol**

Aggie has some lovely
sunflowers.
**Aggie a
de beaux
tournesols.**

surprise   **la surprise**

What a surprise!
Quelle surprise! HOU!

swim   **nager**

Pete can swim very well.
Pete sait très bien nager.

a b c d e f g h i j k l m n o p q r **s** t u v w x y z

swimming pool   la piscine

There are two children in the swimming pool.

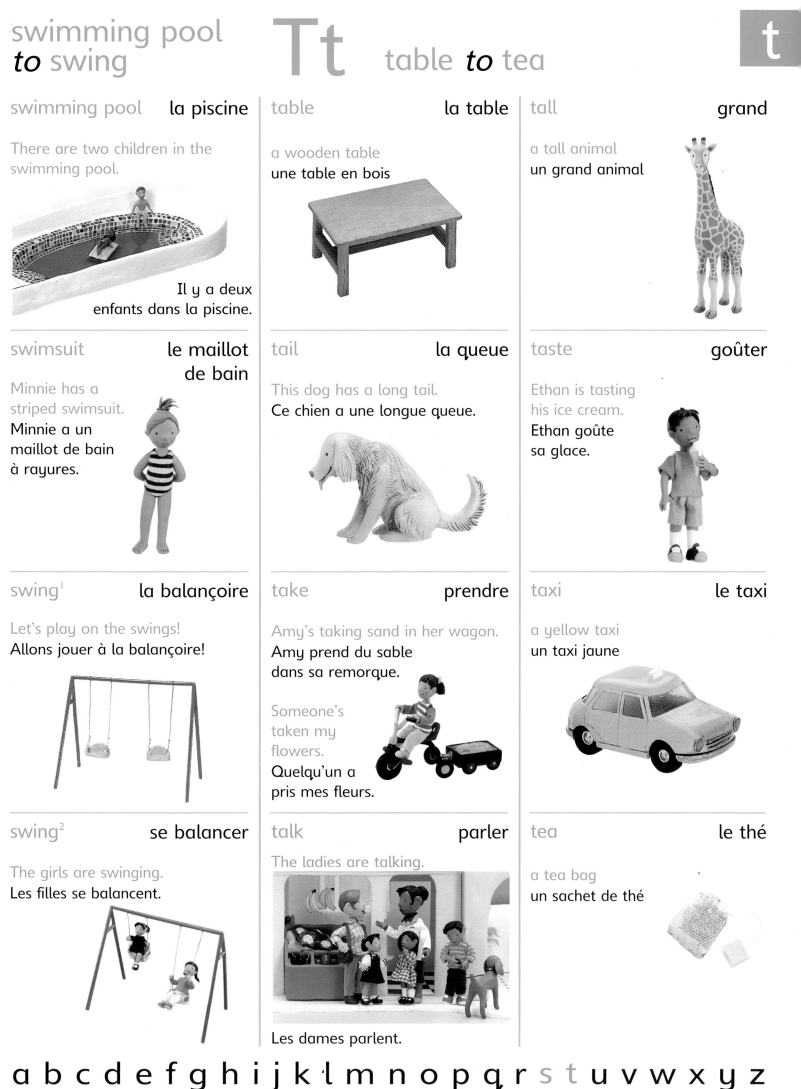

Il y a deux enfants dans la piscine.

swimsuit   le maillot de bain

Minnie has a striped swimsuit.
Minnie a un maillot de bain à rayures.

swing¹   la balançoire

Let's play on the swings!
Allons jouer à la balançoire!

swing²   se balancer

The girls are swinging.
Les filles se balancent.

table   la table

a wooden table
une table en bois

tail   la queue

This dog has a long tail.
Ce chien a une longue queue.

take   prendre

Amy's taking sand in her wagon.
Amy prend du sable dans sa remorque.

Someone's taken my flowers.
Quelqu'un a pris mes fleurs.

talk   parler

The ladies are talking.

Les dames parlent.

tall   grand

a tall animal
un grand animal

taste   goûter

Ethan is tasting his ice cream.
Ethan goûte sa glace.

taxi   le taxi

a yellow taxi
un taxi jaune

tea   le thé

a tea bag
un sachet de thé

a b c d e f g h i j k l m n o p q r s t u v w x y z

teacher	le professeur*, l'instituteur (m), l'institutrice (f)

Our teacher is Mr. Levy.

3 x 3 =

Monsieur Levy est notre instituteur.

team — l'équipe (f)

This is Neil's team.
Voici l'équipe de Neil.

teddy bear — le nounours

This teddy bear has a red scarf.
Ce nounours a une écharpe rouge.

telephone — le téléphone

Where is the telephone, please?
Où est le téléphone, s'il vous plaît?

television — la télévision

There's nothing on television this evening.
Il n'y a rien à la télévision ce soir.

WOW

tell — (explain) raconter, (instruction) dire

Mrs. Beef is telling them the story.
Madame Beef leur raconte l'histoire.

Tell Dad to call me.
Dis à papa de m'appeler.

tent — la tente

Jack has a little, yellow tent.
Jack a une petite tente jaune.

thank — remercier

Polly is thanking Marco for her present.
Polly remercie Marco pour son cadeau.

Merci bien.

thin	(person, animal) maigre (line) fin

a thin cat
un chat maigre

thin string
de la corde fine

thing — la chose

Tina still has some things to do.

Tina a encore des choses à faire.

think — (believe) croire, (consider) penser

I think he is ready.
Je crois qu'il est prêt.

Maddy thinks spiders are horrible
Maddy pense que les araignées sont horribles.

(to be) thirsty — avoir soif

Polly is very thirsty.
Polly a très soif.

a b c d e f g h i j k l m n o p q r s **t** u v w x y z

* A *professeur* teaches children aged 12 and above, and an *instituteur* or *institutrice* teaches younger children.

through — par

Mr. Bun is going out through the front door.
Monsieur Bun sort par la porte d'entrée.

tie — nouer

Someone has tied the ribbons.
Quelqu'un a noué les rubans.

tip — le bout

The tip of the fox's tail is white.

Le bout de la queue du renard est blanc.

throw — jeter

Anna is throwing the ball to Jack.
Anna jette la balle à Jack.

tiger — le tigre

Tigers live in Asia.
Les tigres vivent en Asie.

toast — le toast

The toast is ready.
Les toasts sont prêts.

thumb — le pouce

This is Polly's thumb.
Voici le pouce de Polly.

time (on a clock) l'heure (f), (time taken) le temps

What time is it?
Quelle heure est-il?

The journey doesn't take much time.
Le voyage ne prend pas beaucoup de temps.

toddler — le petit enfant

Joshua is only a toddler.
Joshua n'est qu'un petit enfant.

ticket — le billet, (bus, subway) le ticket

I've already bought my ticket.
J'ai déjà acheté mon billet.

tiny — minuscule

a small cat and a tiny cat

un petit chat et un chat minuscule

toe — l'orteil (m) *or* le doigt de pied

Toes are at the end of feet.
Les orteils sont au bout des pieds.

a b c d e f g h i j k l m n o p q r s **t** u v w x y z

together ensemble

Jenny and Ethan are playing together.
Jenny et Ethan jouent ensemble.

tonight ce soir

Je vais au théâtre ce soir.

She's going to the theater tonight.

top le haut, (on top) sur

I have a blue top.
J'ai un haut bleu.

The kitten is on top of the desk.
Le chaton est sur le bureau.

toilet les WC (m), (restroom) les toilettes (f)

There is a toilet in the blue bathroom.
Il y a des WC dans la salle de bains bleue.

tooth la dent

Zach is showing his teeth.
Zach montre ses dents.

touch toucher

The label says "Please do not touch."

Ne pas toucher SVP

tomato la tomate

a nice, ripe tomato
une belle tomate mûre

toothbrush la brosse à dents

This is Zach's toothbrush.

Voici la brosse à dents de Zach.

towel la serviette

Anna has a big, blue towel.
Anna a une grande serviette bleue.

tongue la langue

Luke is sticking his tongue out.
Luke tire la langue.

toothpaste le dentifrice

mint toothpaste
du dentifrice à la menthe.

town la ville

This is the town center.
Voici le centre de la ville.

a b c d e f g h i j k l m n o p q r s t u v w x y z

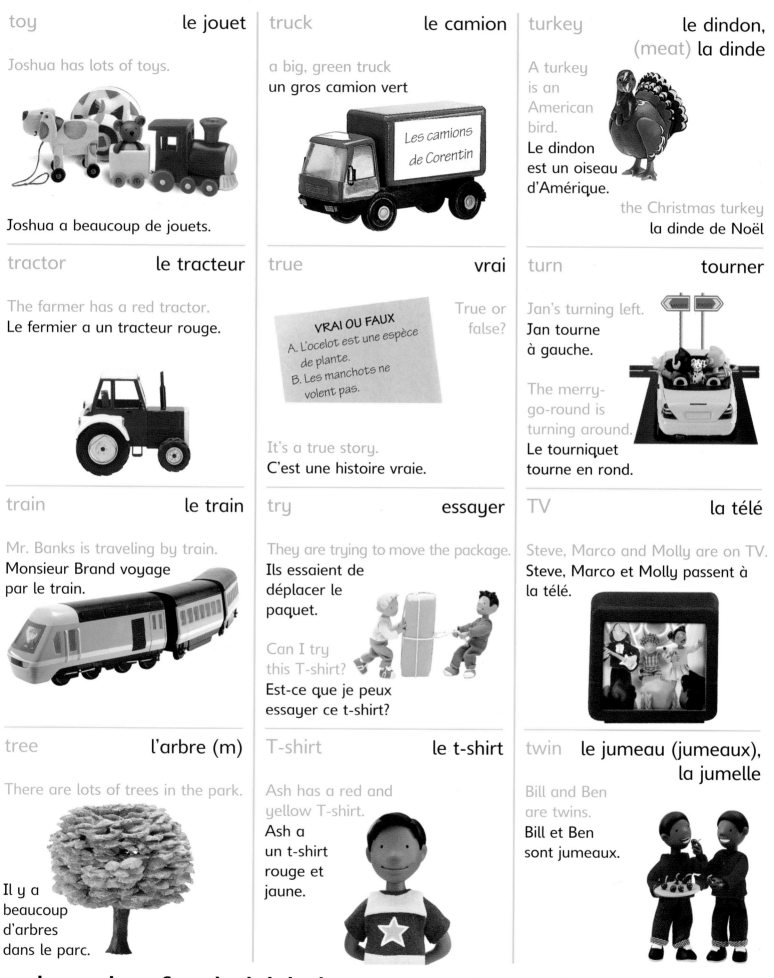

toy — le jouet

Joshua has lots of toys.
Joshua a beaucoup de jouets.

tractor — le tracteur

The farmer has a red tractor.
Le fermier a un tracteur rouge.

train — le train

Mr. Banks is traveling by train.
Monsieur Brand voyage par le train.

tree — l'arbre (m)

There are lots of trees in the park.
Il y a beaucoup d'arbres dans le parc.

truck — le camion

a big, green truck
un gros camion vert

Les camions de Corentin

true — vrai

VRAI OU FAUX
A. L'ocelot est une espèce de plante.
B. Les manchots ne volent pas.

True or false?

It's a true story.
C'est une histoire vraie.

try — essayer

They are trying to move the package.
Ils essaient de déplacer le paquet.

Can I try this T-shirt?
Est-ce que je peux essayer ce t-shirt?

T-shirt — le t-shirt

Ash has a red and yellow T-shirt.
Ash a un t-shirt rouge et jaune.

turkey — le dindon, (meat) la dinde

A turkey is an American bird.
Le dindon est un oiseau d'Amérique.

the Christmas turkey
la dinde de Noël

turn — tourner

Jan's turning left.
Jan tourne à gauche.

The merry-go-round is turning around.
Le tourniquet tourne en rond.

TV — la télé

Steve, Marco and Molly are on TV.
Steve, Marco et Molly passent à la télé.

twin — le jumeau (jumeaux), la jumelle

Bill and Ben are twins.
Bill et Ben sont jumeaux.

a b c d e f g h i j k l m n o p q r s t u v w x y z

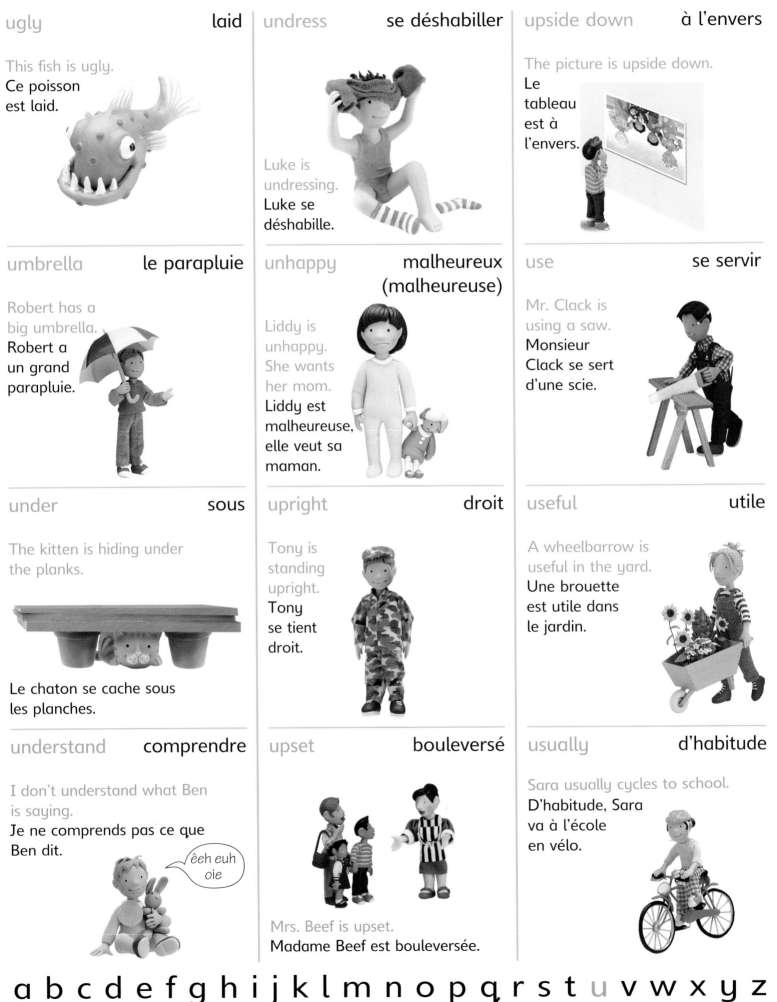

ugly — laid

This fish is ugly.
Ce poisson est laid.

umbrella — le parapluie

Robert has a big umbrella.
Robert a un grand parapluie.

under — sous

The kitten is hiding under the planks.
Le chaton se cache sous les planches.

understand — comprendre

I don't understand what Ben is saying.
Je ne comprends pas ce que Ben dit.

êeh euh oie

undress — se déshabiller

Luke is undressing.
Luke se déshabille.

unhappy — malheureux (malheureuse)

Liddy is unhappy. She wants her mom.
Liddy est malheureuse, elle veut sa maman.

upright — droit

Tony is standing upright.
Tony se tient droit.

upset — bouleversé

Mrs. Beef is upset.
Madame Beef est bouleversée.

upside down — à l'envers

The picture is upside down.
Le tableau est à l'envers.

use — se servir

Mr. Clack is using a saw.
Monsieur Clack se sert d'une scie.

useful — utile

A wheelbarrow is useful in the yard.
Une brouette est utile dans le jardin.

usually — d'habitude

Sara usually cycles to school.
D'habitude, Sara va à l'école en vélo.

a b c d e f g h i j k l m n o p q r s t **u** v w x y z

vacuum cleaner l'aspirateur (m)

Can I borrow the vacuum cleaner?

Est-ce que je peux emprunter l'aspirateur?

vase le vase

a vase of flowers

un vase de fleurs

vegetable le légume

different vegetables

différents légumes

very très

Flora is dirty and Sally is very dirty.

Flora est sale et Sally est très sale.

view la vue

a nice view of the country

une belle vue sur la campagne

visit visiter

The children are visiting the museum.

Les enfants visitent le musée.

visitor l'invité (m) l'invitée (f)

The visitors are arriving.

Les invités arrivent.

voice la voix

Molly has a lovely voice.

Laaaaaa!

Molly a une belle voix.

wait attendre

They are waiting for the bus.

Ils attendent le bus.

waiter le serveur

The waiter is bringing a cup of tea.

Le serveur apporte un thé.

waitress la serveuse

The waitress is bringing two cups of coffee.

La serveuse apporte deux cafés.

wake (someone) réveiller, (wake up) se réveiller

Sam is just waking.

Sam se réveille juste.

a b c d e f g h i j k l m n o p q r s t u v w x y z

walk marcher, (go on foot) aller à pied

Danny is walking fast.
Danny marche vite.

He walks to school.
Il va à l'école à pied.

wall le mur

The hens are on a stone wall.
Les poules sont sur un mur de pierre.

want vouloir

Jenny wants some more wagons.
Jenny veut encore des wagons.

warm chaud

Renata has a nice, warm coat.
Renata a un manteau bien chaud.

wash laver, (yourself) se laver

Jack is washing.
Jack se lave.

washing machine la machine à laver

a new washing machine
une machine à laver neuve

watch[1] la montre

Polly has a new watch for her birthday.
Polly a une montre neuve pour son anniversaire.

watch[2] regarder

They are all watching the clown.
Ils regardent tous le clown.

water l'eau (f) (eaux)

Becky is playing in the warm water.
Becky joue dans l'eau chaude.

wave[1] la vague

a big wave **une grosse vague**

wave[2] saluer

Polly is waving to her friends.
Polly salue ses amis.

way (route) le chemin, (method) la façon

the way to the town
le chemin de la ville

a way of cooking eggs
une façon de faire cuire les œufs

a b c d e f g h i j k l m n o p q r s t u v w x y z

wear   **porter**

Miriam is wearing a red suit.
Miriam porte un tailleur rouge.

weather   **le temps**

winter weather
temps d'hiver

web   **la toile,**
(World Wide) Web   **le Web**

a spider's web
une toile d'araignée

a Web site
un site Web

week   **la semaine**

the days of the week
les jours de la semaine

lundi
mardi
mercredi
jeudi
vendredi
samedi
dimanche

well   **bien**

How are you?
I'm very well, thank you.
Comment ça va?
Très bien, merci.

Sara reads very well.
Sara lit très bien.

wet   **mouillé**

Joe the plumber is all wet.
Joe, le plombier, est tout mouillé.

whale   **la baleine,**
(killer whale)   **l'orque (m)**

Killer whales swim very fast.

Les orques nagent très vite.

wheel   **la roue**

This is a big truck wheel.
Voici une grosse roue de camion.

while   **pendant que**

While his parents are talking, Jack is eating a muffin.
Pendant que ses parents parlent, Jack mange un gâteau.

wide   **large**

The sofa is fairly wide.

Le canapé est assez large.

wild   **sauvage**

wild animals

des animaux sauvages

win   **gagner**

The pink cake has won first prize.
Le gâteau rose a gagné le premier prix.

a b c d e f g h i j k l m n o p q r s t u v w x y z

wind — le vent

a windy day
un jour de vent

window — la fenêtre

Look out of the window.
Regarde par la fenêtre.

wish — le vœu (vœux)

The fairy can give three wishes.

La fée donne trois vœux.

witch — la sorcière

There are often witches in fairy tales.
Il y a souvent des sorcières dans les contes de fées.

with — avec, à

Ben sleeps with his teddy bear.
Ben dort avec son nounours.

a bird with blue feet
un oiseau aux pattes bleues

woman — la femme

This woman is a gardener.
Cette femme est jardinière.

wood — le bois

This table is made of wood.
Cette table est en bois.

There are woods beside the lake.
Il y a des bois à côté du lac.

word — le mot

a list of words
une liste de mots

adresse
brillant
comment
dess
enveloppe

work — (do a job) travailler, (function) marcher

Mick works all day.
Mick travaille toute la journée.

This computer doesn't work.
Cet ordinateur ne marche pas.

world — le monde

all the countries in the world
tous les pays du monde

write — écrire

Oliver is writing his first name.
Oliver écrit son prénom.

OLIVER

wrong — mauvais

the wrong answers
les mauvaises réponses

2 + 3 = 7   X
4 + 6 = 9   X
5 − 3 = 4   X

a b c d e f g h i j k l m n o p q r s t u v w x y z

Xx

Yy

Zz

---

x   (kiss) **bisou**
(in sums) **x**

Love Olivia xxx
Bisous Olivia

$$2 \times 2 = 4$$

(two times two equals four)
(deux fois deux égale quatre)

Xmas   **Noël**

Happy Xmas!
Joyeux Noël!

---

x-ray   **le rayon x,**
(photo) **la radiographie**

The x-ray shows Robert's skeleton.
La radiographie montre la squelette de Robert.

---

xylophone   **le xylophone**

This xylophone has six notes.
Ce xylophone a six notes.

---

yawn   **bâiller**

Sam's yawning.
Sam bâille.

---

year   **l'an (m), l'année (f)**

Flora is five years old. Annie is a year older.
Flora a cinq ans. Annie a un an de plus.

the days of the year
les jours de l'année

---

yet   **encore**

Ben can't walk yet.
Ben ne sait pas encore marcher.

---

young   **jeune**

young children
des enfants jeunes

---

zebra   **le zèbre**

Zebras live in Africa.
Les zèbres vivent en Afrique.

---

zero   **zéro**

Five take away five equals zero.
Cinq moins cinq égale zéro.

$$5 - 5 = 0$$

---

zipper   **la fermeture éclair**

This zipper is half open.
Cette fermeture éclair est à moitié ouverte.

---

zoo   **le zoo**

There's a panda at the zoo.
Il y a un panda au zoo.

a b c d e f g h i j k l m n o p q r s t u v w x y z

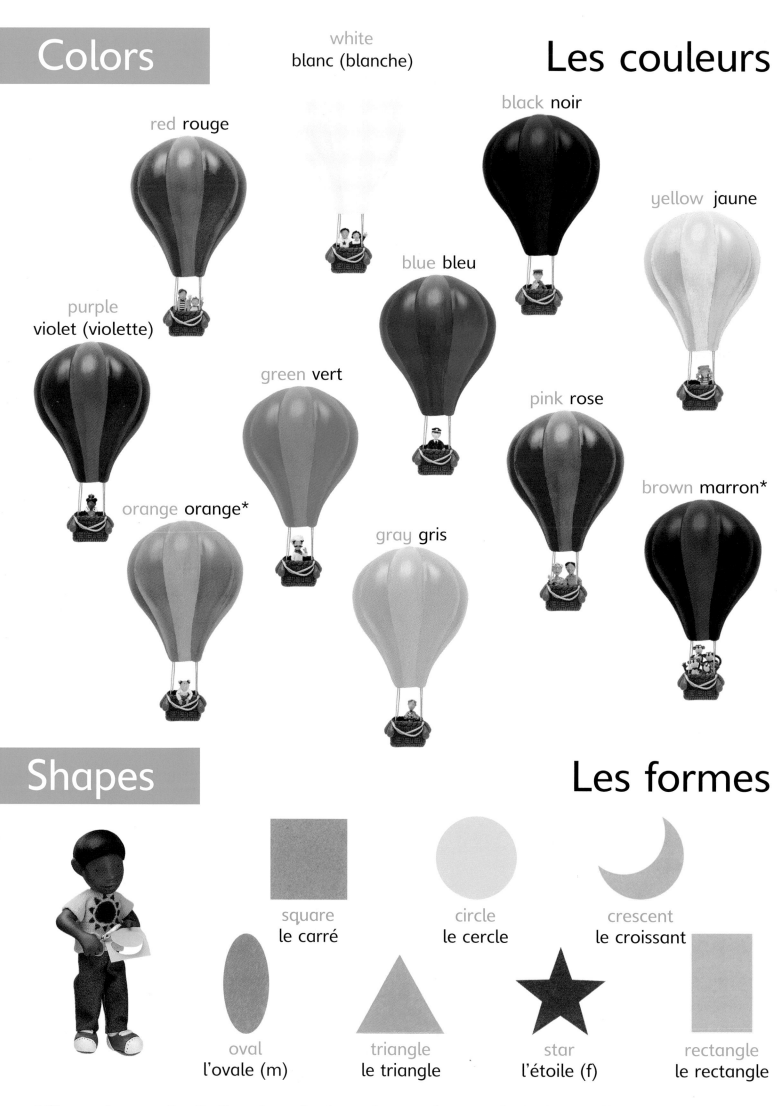

Colors

Les couleurs

white
blanc (blanche)

red rouge

black noir

yellow jaune

blue bleu

purple
violet (violette)

green vert

pink rose

orange orange*

gray gris

brown marron*

Shapes

Les formes

square
le carré

circle
le cercle

crescent
le croissant

oval
l'ovale (m)

triangle
le triangle

star
l'étoile (f)

rectangle
le rectangle

* These colors aren't quite like other adjectives - they are the same for both masculine and feminine, and they don't add *s* for plurals: a brown shoe une chassure marron; orange fruit des fruits orange.

Numbers

1st 1er (1ère)
2nd 2ème
3rd 3ème
4th 4ème
5th 5ème
6th 6ème
7th 7ème
8th 8ème
9th 9ème
10th 10ème

premier
(première) deuxième troisième quatrième cinquième sixième septième huitième neuvième dixième

1	un (une)	
2	deux	
3	trois	
4	quatre	
5	cinq	
6	six	
7	sept	
8	huit	
9	neuf	
10	dix	
11	onze	
12	douze	
13	treize	
14	quatorze	
15	quinze	
16	seize	
17	dix-sept	
18	dix-huit	
19	dix-neuf	
20	vingt	

30	40	50	60	70	80	90	100	1000
trente	quarante	cinquante	soixante	soixante-dix	quatre-vingts	quatre-vingt-dix	cent	mille

Days and months

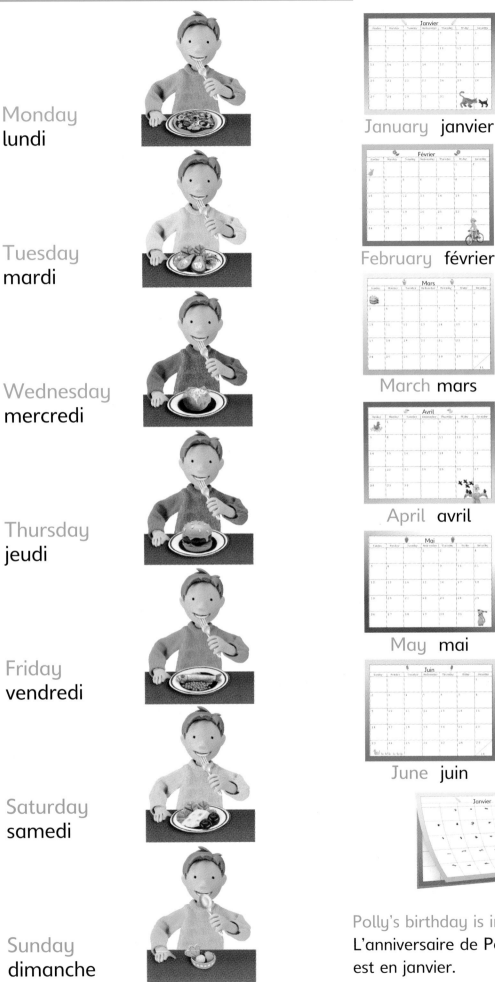

Monday
lundi

Tuesday
mardi

Wednesday
mercredi

Thursday
jeudi

Friday
vendredi

Saturday
samedi

Sunday
dimanche

Les jours et les mois

January janvier

February février

March mars

April avril

May mai

June juin

July juillet

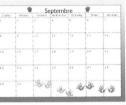

August août

September septembre

October octobre

November novembre

December décembre

Polly's birthday is in January.
L'anniversaire de Polly
est en janvier.

Les saisons

Spring le printemps

Summer l'été

Fall l'automne

Winter l'hiver

Family

La famille

Polly's photo album
l'album photos de Polly

sister, brother
la soeur, le frère

father
le père

mother
la mère

Dad
Papa

Mom
Maman

son
le fils

daughter
la fille

Dad and his brother
Papa et son frère

baby
le bébé

grandmother
la grand-mère

grandfather
le grand-père

Grandma
Mamie

grandchildren
les petits-enfants

Grandpa
Papi

aunt
la tante

(girl) cousin
la cousine*

uncle
l'oncle (m)

grandparents
les grands-parents

children
les enfants

parents
les parents

* boy cousin would be *le cousin*.

Words we use a lot

On these pages you'll find some words that are useful for making sentences, and are used in sentences in the dictionary. Remember that in French some words can change, depending on whether the word that follows is masculine or feminine, singular or plural (see page 3). You'll find a little more about how words like *de* and *à* change on pages 96 and 100.

about	(story) **sur**
	(more or less) **environ**
across	**à travers**
again	**encore**
almost	**presque**
also	**aussi**
always	**toujours**
and	**et**
another	**un autre,**
	une autre
around	**autour de**
because	**parce que**
but	**mais**
by	(beside) **à côté de**
	(done by) **par**
each *or* every	**chaque**
	or **tout, toute**
everybody	
or everyone	**tout le monde**
everything	**tout**
everywhere	**partout**
for	**pour**
he	**il**
her	(belonging to...) **son,**
	sa, ses
	(to, for...) **la** *or* **lui**
here	**ici**
here's	**voici**
him	**le** *or* **lui**
his	(belonging to...) **son,**
	sa, ses
I	**je**
if	**si**
in, into	**dans** *or* **en**
it	**il, elle**

its	**son, sa, ses**
it's	**c'est**
just	**seulement**
me	**me** *or* **moi**
my	**mon, ma, mes**
myself	**moi-même**
no	(not yes) **non**
	(not one) **aucun, aucune**
none	**aucun, aucune**
of	**de**
on	(on top of) **sur**
	(wall, radio...) **à**
	(bicycle, vacation...) **en**
or	**ou**
our	**notre, nos**
out of	**hors de**
she	**elle**
so	(so big) **si**
	(because of this) **donc**
somebody	**quelqu'un,**
or someone	**quelqu'une**
something	**quelque chose**
sometimes	**parfois**
somewhere	**quelque part**
than	**que**
that	**cela**
their	**leur, leurs**
them	**eux, elles**
	(to, for...) **les** *or* **leur**
then	**ensuite** *or* **puis**
there	**là**
there's	**il y a**
they	**ils, elles**
today	**aujourd'hui**

tomorrow	**demain**
too	**aussi**
unless	**sauf si**
	or **à moins que**
until	**jusqu'à**
us	**nous**
we	**nous**
what	**ce que**
	(in questions) **que**
which	**que**
	(in questions) **quel,**
	quelle, quels, quelles
whose	**dont**
	(in questions) **à qui**
yes	(agreeing) **oui**
	(contradicting) **si**
yesterday	**hier**
you	**tu** *or* **vous***
	(to, for...) **te** *or* **toi**
	or **vous***
your	**ton, ta, tes**
	or **votre, vos**

* For the difference between *tu* and *vous*, see page 4.

This, these

On page 3, you can see how the word for "the" changes, depending whether a noun is masculine or feminine. The word for "this" is *ce*, and it changes in a similar way:

the boy	le garçon
this boy	ce garçon
the word	le mot
this word	ce mot

If the following noun is masculine and begins with *a, e, i, o* or *u* (and sometimes *h*), *ce* becomes *cet*:

the tree	l'arbre
this tree	cet arbre
the man	l'homme
this man	cet homme

For all feminine nouns, you use *cette*:

the woman	la femme
this woman	cette femme
the island	l'île
this island	cette île

When you are talking about more than one of something (plurals), the word for "these" is *ces*, whether the following noun is masculine or feminine:

the boys	les garçons
these boys	ces garçons
the words	les mots
these words	ces mots
the trees	les arbres
these trees	ces arbres
the men	les hommes
these men	ces hommes
the women	les femmes
these women	ces femmes
the islands	les îles
these islands	ces îles

One, some, all

In French, the words for "one", "some" and "all" can change, depending on whether the following noun is masculine or feminine, singular or plural (see page 3). The word for "a" or "an" is the same as the word for "one":

a boy *or* one boy	un garçon
a girl *or* one girl	une fille

The word for "some" is *de*, but if the following noun is masculine, this changes to *du*. If the following noun begins with *a, e, i, o* or *u* and sometimes *h,* it changes to *de l'*:

some bread	du pain
some money	de l'argent
some jelly	de la confiture

If you are talking about more than one, *de* changes to *des*, whether the noun is masculine or feminine:

some boys	des garçons
some girls	des filles

The word for "all" is *tout*, or *toute* in the feminine:

all the time	tout le temps
all day	toute la journée

When you are talking about more than one, it becomes *tous* for masculine nouns and *toutes* for feminine nouns:

all the boys	tous les garçons
all the words	tous les mots
all the trees	tous les arbres
all the girls	toutes les filles
all the women	toutes les femmes
all the islands	toutes les îles

Making sentences

To make sentences in French, you usually put the words in the same order as in an English sentence. Remember to make any changes you need for masculine or feminine words in the sentence. Here are some examples from the dictionary:

The bus arrives at noon.
Le bus arrive à midi.

The kitten is behind the flowerpot.
Le chaton est derrière le pot de fleurs.

Bill is close to Ben.
Bill est près de Ben.

Where does the adjective go?

In English, adjectives usually go before the noun they are describing. In French, most adjectives go after the noun:

The baker sells fresh bread.
Le boulanger vend du pain frais.

a dangerous snake
un serpent dangereux

Becky has green ribbons.
Becky a des rubans verts.

However, some very common adjectives, such as *beau, bon, grand, joli, mauvais, nouveau, petit* and *vieux*, do go before the noun:

a large amount of pasta
une grande quantité de pâtes

Ruth has a pretty necklace.
Ruth a un joli collier.

It is possible to have adjectives before and after a noun:

Renata has a lovely red coat.
Renata a un beau manteau rouge.

a nice, sweet, green pear
une belle poire verte sucrée

More and most

In English, when you compare things, you often add "er" to an adjective: "A mouse is smaller than a rabbit." Other times, you use "more": "My puzzle is more difficult than yours." In French, you use the word *plus* to compare things:

Bushes are smaller than trees.
Les buissons sont plus petits que les arbres.

The car is more expensive than the duck.
La voiture est plus chère que le canard.

Mountains are higher than hills.
Les montagnes sont plus hautes que les collines.

When you compare several things, in English you add "est" to the adjective, or use "most": "This tree's the tallest." "This is the most delicious." In French, you use *le plus,* (or *la plus* or *les plus*):

Ben is the youngest.
Ben est le plus jeune.

This coat is the most expensive.
Cette robe est la plus chère.

As in English, you have special words for:

better	mieux
the best	le meilleur (la meilleure, les meilleurs, les meilleures)
worse	pire
the worst	le pire (la pire, les pires)

(you can also use *plus mauvais*)

My plane is better than your truck.
Mon avion est mieux que ton camion.

the best in the class
le meilleur *or* la meilleure de la classe

the worst place to have a picnic
le pire endroit pour faire un pique-nique

Making questions

The easiest questions in French are questions you answer "yes" or "no" to. The easiest way to make a sentence into this kind of question is to add the words *Est-ce que* at the beginning. For example:

Is the bus going into town?
Est-ce que le bus va en ville?

Is the kitten behind the flowerpot?
Est-ce que le chaton est derrière le pot de fleurs?

Is Bill close to Ben?
Est-ce que Bill est près de Ben?

Is Oliver hungry?
Est-ce qu'Oliver a faim?

You can also make questions beginning with question words, such as:

Who..?	Qui..?
What..?	Que..?
Where..?	Où..?
When..?	Quand..?
Why..?	Pourquoi..?
How..?	Comment..?
How many..?	
or How much?	Combien..?

The verb usually comes after the question word, as it does in English:

Who wants some cake?
Qui veut du gâteau?

What does this word mean?
Que veut dire ce mot?

Where is the kitten?
Où est le chaton?

How is Beth feeling?
Comment se sent Beth?

How many apples are there?
Combien y a-t-il de pommes?

How much do the apples cost?
Combien coûtent les pommes?

You can also use *est-ce que* after question words. For example:

What's happening here?
Qu'est-ce qu'il se passe ici?

What's she saying?
Qu'est-ce qu'elle dit?

When does the bus arrive?
Quand est-ce que le bus arrive?

Why is Ross crying?
Pourquoi est-ce que Ross pleure?

How does she know that?
Comment est-ce qu'elle sait cela?

The word for "Which..?" changes, depending on whether the word it goes with is masculine or feminine, singular or plural:

Which bike goes faster?
Quel vélo va plus vite?

Which is the biggest house?
Quelle est la maison la plus grande?

Which toys are the cheapest?
Quels jouets sont les moins chers?

Which girls are playing tennis?
Quelles filles jouent au tennis?

There are some useful words for questions which mostly begin "any–" in English:

anybody *or* anyone	quelqu'un
anything	quelque chose
anywhere	quelque part

For example:

Is there anybody at home?
Est-ce qu'il y a quelqu'un à la maison?

Is anyone going into town?
Est-ce que quelqu'un va en ville?

Does she need anything?
Est-ce qu'elle a besoin de quelque chose?

Can you see my glasses anywhere?
Est-ce que tu vois mes lunettes quelque part?

Negative sentences

A negative sentence is a "not" sentence, such as "I'm not hungry". You usually make a sentence negative in French by adding *ne... pas* around the verb (or *n'.... pas* if the verb begins with *a, e, i, o, u,* and sometimes *h*):

The bus isn't going into town.
Le bus ne va pas en ville.

The kitten isn't behind the flowerpot.
Le chaton n'est pas derrière le pot de fleurs.

Bill isn't close to Ben.
Bill n'est pas près de Ben.

Oliver's not hungry.
Oliver n'a pas faim.

If there is more than one verb, you only make one negative, as in English:

He doesn't like doing his homework.
Il n'aime pas faire ses devoirs.

If the sentence includes "any", or has the meaning "any", this becomes *de (or d'* before *a, e, i, o, u* and sometimes *h*):

Mom doesn't want any pie.
Maman ne veut pas de tarte.

I don't see any trees.
Je ne vois pas d'arbres.

Ethan doesn't have any other toys.
Ethan n'a pas d'autres jouets.

I don't have a cat (I don't have any cats).
Je n'ai pas de chat.

He doesn't eat bread
(He doesn't eat any bread).
Il ne mange pas de pain.

De doesn't change, whether the word following is masculine or feminine, singular or plural:

I don't need any milk.
Je n'ai pas besoin de lait.

She doesn't have any tickets.
Elle n'a pas de billets.

There are some useful words for negative sentences which mostly begin "no–" in English (it's the same as saying "not any–"):

nobody *or* no one	personne
nothing	rien
nowhere	nulle part
never	jamais
no more	plus

You use these in the place of *pas* in a simple negative sentence like the ones on the left. For example:

There is nobody at home
or There isn't anybody at home.
Il n'y a personne à la maison.

I have nothing to eat
or I don't have anything to eat.
Je n'ai rien à manger.

This path goes nowhere
or This path doesn't go anywhere.
Ce sentier ne va nulle part.

The train is never late
or The train isn't ever late.
Le train n'est jamais en retard.

She has no more fruit
or She doesn't have any more fruit.
Elle n'a plus de fruits.

When you hear French people speaking, especially children, you'll notice that they often leave out the *ne...* You might hear:

"There's nobody at home."
"Y a personne à la maison."

"I've nothing to eat"
"J'ai rien à manger."

"She has no more fruit."
"Elle a plus de fruits."

If you are writing French, though, you must keep the *ne...* in the sentence.

To, from and other useful place words

The French word for "to" (and also "at") is *à*. If it is followed by a masculine noun, it changes to *au* (*à l'* for nouns beginning with *a, e, i, o* or *u* and sometimes *h*):

I'm going to the supermarket.
Je vais au supermarché.

He is at the workshop.
Il est à l'atelier.

The children are at school.
Les enfants sont à l'école.

She is going to the beach.
Elle va à la plage.

If the following noun is plural, *à* changes to *aux*, whether the noun is masculine or feminine:

I am giving some apples to the boys.
Je donne des pommes aux garçons.

Mr. Levy is explaining to the pupils.
Monsieur Levy explique aux élèves.

She is feeding corn to the hens.
Elle donne du maïs aux poules.

In French, there is also a special word *chez*, meaning "at somebody's house or store". For example:

Jenny's going to Ethan's house.
Jenny va chez Ethan.

Polly is at her grandparents' (house).
Polly est chez ses grands-parents.

I'm going to the butcher's (store).
Je vais chez le boucher.

There isn't a special word for "home" in French, so you use *chez* instead:

I'm going home.
Je vais chez moi.

We're at home this evening.
Nous sommes chez nous ce soir.

The French word for "from" (and also "of") is *de*, which you also saw on page 96, meaning "some". It changes in the same way when you use it to mean "from" or "of":

He's coming from the office.
Il vient du bureau.

the bark of the tree
l'écorce de l'arbre

I'm taking a book from the shelf.
Je prends un livre de l'étagère.

the meaning of the words
le sens des mots

the wheels of the cars
les roues des voitures

De is also part of lots of other useful place expressions:

next to	à côté de
near to	près de
a long way from	loin de
at the top of	en haut de
at the bottom of	en bas de
above	au-dessus de
beneath	au-dessous de

For example:

The kitten is next to the flowerpot.
Le chaton est à côté du pot de fleurs.

The store is near the swimming pool.
Le magasin est près de la piscine.

The house is a long way from the school.
La maison est loin de l'école.

The kitten is at the top of the stairs.
Le chaton est en haut de l'escalier.

The clock is above the cupboard.
La pendule est au-dessus du placard.

The radiator is beneath the window.
Le radiateur est au-dessous de la fenêtre.

Verbs

These pages list the verbs (or "doing" words) that appear in the main part of the dictionary. Page 4 explains a little about verbs in French, and how the endings change for "I", "you", "he" or "she", and so on. It also introduces the useful verbs *avoir* and *être*.

   In this list, you can find some of the most useful forms of the verb: the infinitive (the "to" form) and the "he" form (*il* in French. The "she" or *elle* form is the same). The "I" or *je* form is usually the same as the "he" or *il* form. To make the "they" (*ils* or *elles*) form you usually add *–nt* or *–ent* at the end. If these forms are any different, they are shown in this list. They are in the present, which is the form you use to talk about what is happening now.

All the verbs marked with an asterisk (*) are a type of verb called a "reflexive verb". They are often used where you would use "... myself", "... yourself", and so on, in English. The main part of the verb works like other verbs, but you also need to change the *se* at the beginning, depending on who is doing the action. For example, *se laver* ("to wash yourself") is formed like this:

I wash myself	je me lave
you wash yourself	tu te laves
he washes himself	il se lave
she washes herself	elle se lave
we wash ourselves	nous nous lavons
you wash yourselves	vous vous lavez
they wash themselves	ils *or* elles se lavent

aboyer	to bark	aller	to go
il aboie		je vais	
		il va	
accrocher	to hang up	ils vont	
il accroche			
		*s'amuser	to enjoy
		je m'amuse	yourself
acheter	to buy	il s'amuse	
il achète			
		appartenir	to belong
adorer	to love	j'appartiens	
il adore		il appartient	
		ils appartiennent	
*s'agenouiller	to kneel		
je m'agenouille	down	appeler	to call
il s'agenouille		il appelle	
aider	to help	apporter	to bring
il aide		il apporte	
aimer	to enjoy,	apprendre	to learn
il aime	to like, to love	j'apprends	
		il apprend	
ajouter	to add	ils apprennent	
il ajoute			

appuyer	to press	attendre	to wait
il appuie		j'attends	
		il attend	
arrêter	to stop		
il arrête		attraper	to catch
		il attrape	
*s'arrêter	to stop		
je m'arrête	(yourself)	bâiller	to yawn
il s'arrête		il bâille	
arriver	to arrive,	*se balancer	to swing
il arrive	to reach,	je me balance	
	to happen	il se balance	
*s'asseoir	to sit down	balayer	to sweep
je m'assieds		il balaie	
il s'assied			
ils s'asseyent		*se battre	to fight
		je me bats	
attacher	to join,	il se bat	
il attache	to attach	ils se battent	
atteindre	to reach	boire	to drink
j'atteins		je bois	
il atteint		il boit	
ils atteignent		ils boivent	

Verbs

bouger — to move
il bouge

brûler — to burn
il brûle

buter — to bump
il bute

cacher — to hide (something)
il cache

*se cacher — to hide (yourself)
je me cache
il se cache

cancaner — to quack
il cancane

casser — to break
il casse

chanter — to sing
il chante

chauffer — to heat
il chauffe

chercher — to search
il cherche

choisir — to choose
je choisis
il choisit
ils choisissent

coller — to stick
il colle

commencer — to begin, to start
il commence

comprendre — to understand
je comprends
il comprend
ils comprennent

conduire — to drive
je conduis
il conduit
ils conduisent

congeler — to freeze
il congèle

connaître — to know (people)
je connais
il connaît
ils connaissent

construire — to build
je construis
il construit
ils construisent

contenir — to contain
je contiens
il contient
ils contiennent

copier — to copy
il copie

*se coucher — to lie down
je me couche
il se couche

coudre — to sew
je couds
il coud
ils cousent

couler — to sink
il coule

couper — to cut
il coupe

courir — to run
je cours
il court
ils courent

creuser — to dig
il creuse

croire — to think, to believe
je crois
il croit
ils croient

croquer — to bite (food)
il croque

cueillir — to pick
il cueille

danser — to dance
il danse

découper — to cut out
il découpe

demander — to ask
il demande

démanger — to itch
il démange

*se dépêcher — to hurry
je me dépêche
il se dépêche

dépenser — to spend
il dépense

déplacer — to move
il déplace

déranger — to bother
il dérange

*se déshabiller — to undress
je me déshabille
il se déshabille

dessiner — to draw
il dessine

détester — to hate
il déteste

deviner — to guess
il devine

dire — to say, to tell
je dis
il dit
ils disent

disparaître — to disappear
je disparaisse
il disparaît
ils disparaissent

donner — to give
il donne

dormir — to sleep
je dors
il dort
ils dorment

*s'échapper — to escape
je m'échappe
il s'échappe

éclabousser — to splash
il éclabousse

économiser — to save
il économise

écrire — to write
j'écris
il écrit
ils écrivent

embrasser — to hug
il embrasse

entendre — to hear
j'entends
il entend

envoyer — to send
il envoie

épeler — to spell
il épèle

essayer — to try
il essaie

étudier — to study
il étudie

expliquer — to explain
il explique

faire — to make, to do
je fais
il fait
ils font

fermer — to close
il ferme

finir — to finish
je finis
il finit
ils finissent

flotter — to float
il flotte

frapper — to hit
il frappe

gagner — to win
il gagne

garder	to keep	jouer	to play	montrer	to show	peindre	to paint
il garde		il joue		il montre		je peins	
						il peint	
garer	to park	laisser	to let,	mordre	to bite	ils peignent	
il gare		il laisse	to leave	je mords			
				il mord		*se pencher	to lean
geler	to freeze	laver	to wash			je me penche	
il gèle		il lave		mourir	to die	il se penche	
				je meurs			
glisser	to slip,	*se laver	to wash	il meurt		pendre	to hang
il glisse	to slide	je me lave	yourself	ils meurent		je pends	
		il se lave				il pend	
*se glisser	to creep			nager	to swim		
je me glisse		lécher	to lick	il nage		penser	to think
il se glisse		il lèche				il pense	
				neiger	to snow		
goûter	to taste	*se lever	to stand up	il neige		percuter	to crash
il goûte		je me lève				il percute	
		il se lève		nettoyer	to clean		
grimper	to climb			il nettoie		perdre	to lose
il grimpe		lire	to read			je perds	
		je lis		nouer	to tie	il perd	
*s'habiller	to dress	il lit		il noue			
je m'habille		ils lisent				piquer	to sting
il s'habille				organiser	to plan	il pique	
		manger	to eat	il organise			
habiter	to live	il mange				pleurer	to cry
il habite				oublier	to forget	il pleure	
		manquer	to be missing	il oublie			
heurter	to bump,	il manque				pleuvoir	to rain
il heurte	to knock			ouvrir	to open	il pleut	
		marcher	to walk,	il ouvre			
hocher (la tête)	to nod	il marche	to work			plier	to fold
il hoche			(machine)	parler	to speak	il plie	
				il parle			
hurler	to shout	mélanger	to mix			plonger	to dive
il hurle		il mélange		partager	to share	il plonge	
				il partage			
indiquer	to point	mener	to lead			porter	to carry,
il indique		il mène		partir	to leave	il porte	to wear
				je pars	(a place)		
*s'inscrire	to join,	mentir	to lie (not	il part		poser	to put down
je m'inscris	become a	je mens	tell truth)			il pose	
il s'inscrit	member	il ment		passer	to pass (give)		
ils s'inscrivent				il passe		poursuivre	to chase
		mesurer	to measure			je poursuis	
inviter	to invite	il mesure		*se passer	to happen	il poursuit	
il invite				il se passe		ils poursuivent	
		mettre	to put				
jeter	to throw	je mets		payer	to pay		
il jette		il met		il paie			
		ils mettent					
jongler	to juggle	monter	to ride a	pêcher	to fish	pousser	to push,
il jongle		il monte	horse	il pêche		il pousse	to grow

Verbs

prendre — to take
je prends
il prend
ils prennent

*se précipiter — to rush
je me précipite
il se précipite

promettre — to promise
je promets
il promet
ils promettent

raccommoder — to mend
il raccommode

raconter — to tell
il raconte

*se rappeler — to remember
je me rappelle
il se rappelle

rater — to miss
il rate

regarder — to look, to watch
il regarde

remarquer — to notice
il remarque

remercier — to thank
il remercie

remplir — to fill
je remplis
il remplit
ils remplissent

remuer — to stir
il remue

rencontrer — to meet
il rencontre

renverser — to spill, to knock over
il renverse

réparer — to fix, to mend
il répare

repérer — to spot
il repère

répondre — to answer
je réponds
il répond

respirer — to breathe
il respire

rester — to stay
il reste

retrouver — to meet
il retrouve

rétrécir — to shrink
je rétrécis
il rétrécit
ils rétrécissent

réussir — to pass (test)
je réussis
il réussit
ils réussissent

réveiller — to wake
il réveille

*se réveiller — to wake up
je me réveille
il se réveille

rire — to laugh
je ris
il rit
ils rient

saluer — to wave
il salue

sauter — to jump
il saute

sauver — to rescue, to save
il sauve

savoir — to know (facts)
je sais
il sait
ils savent

sécher — to dry
il sèche

secouer — to shake
il secoue

sentir — to smell
je sens
il sent

*se sentir — to feel
je me sens
il se sent

*se servir — to use
je me sers
il se sert
ils se servent

signer — to sign
il signe

sonner — to sound, to ring
il sonne

souffler — to blow
il souffle

soulever — to lift
il soulève

sourire — to smile
je souris
il sourit
ils sourient

*se souvenir — to remember
je me souviens
il se souvient
ils se souviennent

tenir — to hold
je tiens
il tient
ils tiennent

tirer — to pull
il tire

tomber — to fall
il tombe

toucher — to touch, to feel
il touche

tourner — to turn
il tourne

travailler — to work
il travaille

traverser — to cross
il traverse

trouver — to find
il trouve

tuer — to kill
il tue

vendre — to sell
je vends
il vend

venir — to come
je viens
il vient
ils viennent

visiter — to visit
il visite

vivre — to live
je vis
il vit
ils vivent

voir — to see
je vois
il voit
ils voient

voler — to fly, to steal
il vole

vouloir — to want
je veux
il veut
ils veulent

*see Reflexive verbs on page 101.

Complete French word list

à	to, with	l'araignée (f)	spider	la batte	bat (for sports)
à côté	beside, next to, by	l'arbre (m)	tree	se battre	to fight
à l'envers	upside down	l'arc-en-ciel (m)	rainbow	le bavoir	bib
à l'intérieur	inside	l'argent (m)	money	beau (bel, belle)	beautiful, nice
à moins que	unless	arrêter	to stop (someone or		(to look at)
à qui	whose (in questions)		something)	beaucoup	a lot, many, much
à travers	across	s'arrêter	to stop (yourself)	le bébé	baby
l'abeille (f)	bee	l'arrière (m)	back (not front)	le bec	beak
abîmé	bad (food)	arriver	to arrive, to come,	la bestiole	bug
aboyer	to bark		to reach, to happen	la betterave	beetroot
accrocher	to hang up	l'art (m)	art	le beurre	butter
acheter	to buy	l'artiste (m or f)	artist	la bicyclette	bicycle
l'acteur (m)	actor	l'aspirateur (m)	vacuum cleaner	bien	well
l'actrice (f)	actress	s'asseoir	to sit down	bien fait	good, well done
adorer	to love (things)	assez	fairly, enough	bien taillé	sharpened
l'adresse (f)	address	l'assiette (f)	plate	bientôt	soon
l'adulte (m or f)	adult	l'astronaute	astronaut	le billet	ticket
l'âge (m)	age	(m or f)		le bisou	kiss
s'agenouiller	to kneel down	attacher	to attach, to join	la blague	joke
l'agneau (m)	lamb	atteindre	to reach	blanc (blanche)	white
aider	to help	attendre	to wait	bleu	blue
l'aigle (m)	eagle	attraper	to catch	le blouson	jacket (men's casual)
l'aiguille (f)	needle	au lieu	instead	boire	to drink
aimer	to love (someone),	au revoir	goodbye	le bois	wood
	to like (something),	aucun or aucune	none, no (not one)	la boîte	box
	to enjoy	au-delà	past	le bol	bowl
l'air (m)	air	au-dessous	beneath	bon (bonne)	good, right
l'aire de jeux (f)	playground	au-dessus	over, above	bon marché	cheap
ajouter	to add	aujourd'hui	today	bonjour	hello
l'album photos	photo album	aussi	also, too	le bord	edge
(m)		l'auto (f)	car	la botte	boot
les aliments (m)	food	l'automne (m)	Fall	la bouche	mouth
aller	to go	autour	around	le boucher	butcher (m)
aller à pied	to walk, go on foot	autre	other	la bouchère	butcher (f)
aller en vélo	to cycle	un or une autre	another	la boue	mud
l'allumette (f)	match	avant	before, front	bouger	to (make a) move
l'alphabet (m)	alphabet	avec	with	la bougie	candle
l'amande (f)	almond	l'averse (f)	shower (rain)	le boulanger	baker (m)
l'ambulance (f)	ambulance	l'avion (m)	plane	la boulangère	baker (f)
l'ami (m)	friend (m)	avoir	to have	bouleversé	upset
l'amie (f)	friend (f)	avoir besoin	to need	boum	bang
amusant	fun	avoir faim	to be hungry	le bout	tip
s'amuser	to enjoy yourself	avoir peur	to be afraid	la bouteille	bottle
l'an (m)	year	avoir soif	to be thirsty	le bouton	button
l'ananas (m)	pineapple	avril	April	la branche	branch
l'âne (m)	donkey			le bras	arm
l'ange (m)	angel	la bague	ring (jewelry)	la brindille	twig, stick
l'animal (m)	animal	la baignoire	bathtub	la brosse	brush, hairbrush
l'animal	pet	bâiller	to yawn	la brosse à dents	toothbrush
domestique (m)		se balancer	to swing	le bruit	noise, sound
l'anneau (m)	ring (shape)	la balançoire	swing	brûler	to burn
l'année (f)	year	balayer	to sweep	bruyant	noisy
l'anniversaire (m)	birthday	la baleine	whale	la bûche	log
août	August	la ballerine	ballerina	le buisson	bush
aplani	level, smooth	le ballon	ball, balloon	le bureau	desk, study
l'appareil photo	camera	la banane	banana	le bus	bus
(m)		la banque	bank	le but	goal
appartenir	to belong	la barbe	beard	buter	to bump
appeler	to call	la barre	bar		
apporter	to bring	la barrière	gate	la cacahuète	peanut
apprendre	to learn	le bas	bottom (not top)	cacher	to hide (something)
appuyer	to press	bas (basse)	low	se cacher	to hide (yourself)
après	after	le bateau	boat	le cadeau	present, gift
l'après-midi	afternoon	le bâtiment	building	le café	café, coffee
(m or f)		le bâton	stick	la cage	cage

le calcul	sum	le chien	dog	le couteau	knife
le camion	truck	le chiffre	number (figure)	le couvercle	lid
la campagne	country, countryside	le chiot	puppy	la couverture	blanket
le canapé	sofa	le chocolat	chocolate	la craie	chalk
le canard	duck	choisir	to choose, to pick	le crayon	pencil
cancaner	to quack	la chose	thing	le crayon cire	crayon
le caneton	duckling	le chou-fleur	cauliflower	creuser	to dig
le carnet	notebook	le ciel	sky	le crocodile	crocodile
la carotte	carrot	cinq	five	croire	to think, to believe
le carré	square	cinquième	fifth	le croissant	crescent
la carte	card, map	cinquante	fifty	la croix	cross (sign)
le casque	helmet	les ciseaux (m)	scissors	croquer	to bite (food)
la casquette	cap	le citron	lemon	cueillir	to pick
casser	to break	la citrouille	pumpkin	la cuillère	spoon
le casse-tête	puzzle	clair	pale, light	la cuisine	kitchen
le CD	CD	la classe	class	curieux (curieuse)	funny, strange, odd
ce	this	la clé, la clef	key	le cygne	swan
ce que	what (not question)	la clenche	(door) handle		
ce soir	tonight	le clou	nail (metal)	la dame	lady
la ceinture	belt	le clown	clown	dangereux (dangereuse)	dangerous
cela	that	la coccinelle	ladybug	dans	in, inside, into
cent	hundred	le cochon d'Inde	guinea pig	danser	to dance
le centre	center	le cœur	heart	la date	date
le cercle	circle	la colle	glue	le dauphin	dolphin
les céréales (f)	cereal	coller	to stick	de	of, from, some
le cerf	deer	le collier	necklace	décembre	December
le cerf-volant	kite	la colline	hill	découper	to cut out
la cerise	cherry	combien	how many, how much	dehors	outside
ces	these			le déjeuner	lunch
c'est	it's	comme	like	délicieux (délicieuse)	delicious
cet (cette)	this	commencer	to begin, to start	demain	tomorrow
la chaise	chair	comment	how	demander	to ask
la chaise haute	highchair	comprendre	to understand	démanger	to itch
la chambre	bedroom	le concombre	cucumber	le demi or la demie	half
le chameau	camel	le concours	quiz	la dent	tooth
le champ	field	conduire	to drive	le dentifrice	toothpaste
le champignon	mushroom	le congélateur	freezer	le or la dentiste	dentist
la chanson	song	congeler	to freeze (something)	se dépêcher	to hurry
chanter	to sing	connaître	to know (people)	dépenser	to spend
le chapeau	hat	construire	to build	déplacer	to move (something)
chaque	each, every	contenir	to hold, to contain	depuis	since
le chat	cat	content	glad, happy	déranger	to bother, to disturb
le château	castle	le contraire	opposite	dernier (dernière)	last
le chaton	kitten	copier	to copy	derrière	behind
chaud	hot, warm	le coquillage	(sea) shell	le derrière	bottom (body)
chauffer	to heat	la coquille	(egg or nut) shell	des	of, from, some
la chaussette	sock	la corde	rope	le désert	desert
le chausson	slipper	le corps	body	se déshabiller	to undress
la chaussure	shoe	le côté	side, edge	le désordre	mess
chauve	bald	le cou	neck	le dessin	drawing
la chauve-souris	bat (animal)	se coucher	to lie down	dessiner	to draw
le chef cuisinier	chef	le coude	elbow	détester	to hate
le chemin	way, route	coudre	to sew	deux	two
la chemise	shirt	couler	to sink	deuxième	second
la chenille	caterpillar	la couleur	color	deviner	to guess
cher (chère)	expensive, dear (in letters)	couper	to cut	d'habitude	usually
		la cour de récréation	playground (school)	le dictionnaire	dictionary
chercher	to search			différent	different
le cheval	horse	courageux (courageuse)	brave	difficile	difficult
le chevalier	knight			dimanche	Sunday
les cheveux (m)	hair	courir	to run	la dinde	turkey (meat)
la cheville	ankle	la couronne	crown	le dindon	turkey (bird)
la chèvre	goat	la course	race		
le chevreau	kid	court	short		
chez	at (someone's home or store)	le cousin	cousin (m)		
		la cousine	cousin (f)		

le dîner	dinner
le dinosaure	dinosaur
dire	to say, to tell (give instructions)
disparaître	to disappear
dix	ten
dix-huit	eighteen
dixième	tenth
dix-neuf	nineteen
dix-sept	seventeen
le doigt	finger
le doigt de pied	toe
donc	so (because of this)
donner	to give
donner à manger	to feed
donner un baiser	to kiss
donner un coup de pied	to kick
dont	whose, of which
doré	golden
dormir	to sleep
le dos	back (body)
la douche	shower (for washing)
doux (douce)	soft, gentle, quiet
douze	twelve
le dragon	dragon
le drap	(bed) sheet
le drapeau	flag
droit	straight, upright
droite	right (not left)
drôle	funny
du	of, from, some
dur	hard
l'eau (f)	water
s'échapper	to escape
l'écharpe (f)	scarf
l'échelle (f)	ladder
éclabousser	to splash
l'école (f)	school
économiser	to save (money or time)
l'écorce (f)	bark (of a tree)
écrire	to write
l'écureuil (m)	squirrel
égal	equal
l'électricité (f)	electricity
l'éléphant (m)	elephant
l'élève (m or f)	pupil
elle	she, it
elles	they, them
l'e-mail (m)	e-mail
embrasser	to hug
l'emploi (m)	job
en	in, into
en bas	down, at the bottom
en face	opposite
en forme	fit
en haut	at the top
en retard	late (not on time)
encore	still, yet, again
endormi	asleep
l'endroit (m)	place
l'enfant (m or f)	child
énorme	enormous
ensemble	together
ensuite	then, next (after that)
entendre	to hear
entre	between
l'enveloppe (f)	envelope
environ	about, more or less
envoyer	to send
l'épaule (f)	shoulder
épeler	to spell
les épinards (m)	spinach
l'éponge (f)	sponge
l'équipe (f)	team, side
l'escalier (m)	stairs
l'escargot (m)	snail
l'espace (m)	space (stars)
l'espèce (f)	sort, type
essayer	to try
et	and
l'étagère (f)	shelf
l'étang (m)	pond
l'été (m)	Summer
l'étoile (f)	star
être	to be
être à genoux	to be kneeling
être à la taille	to fit
être assis	to be sitting
être assorti	to match
être couché	to be lying (down)
être debout	to be standing
être en équilibre	to balance
être important	to matter
étroit	narrow
étudier	to study
eux	them
l'évier (m)	(kitchen) sink
expliquer	to explain
fâché	angry
facile	easy
la façon	way, method
faire	to make, to do, to cook, to bake
faire attention	to watch, to be careful
faire cuire	to cook
faire cuire au four	to bake
faire du camping	to camp
faire du patin	to skate
faire du ski	to ski
faire du vélo	to ride a bicycle
faire face	to face
faire frire	to fry
faire la paire	to match
faire mal	to hurt
faire semblant	to pretend
le fait	fact
la famille	family
le fantôme	ghost
la farine	flour
la faute	mistake
la fée	fairy
la femme	woman
la fenêtre	window
le fer à repasser	iron
la ferme	farm
fermer	to close, to shut
la fermeture éclair	zipper
le fermier	farmer
la fête	party
le feu	fire
la feuille	leaf, sheet (of paper)
février	February
la ficelle	string
la figure	face
la file	line (of people)
le filet	net
la fille	girl, daughter
le fils	son
la fin	end
fin	thin, fine
fini	finished, over
finir	to finish
la flaque	puddle
la fleur	flower
le fleuve	(big) river
flotter	to float
la flûte à bec	recorder
foncé	dark (color)
le foot	soccer
la forêt	forest
la forme	shape
fort	strong, loud
le four à micro-ondes	microwave
la fourchette	fork
la fourmi	ant
la fourrure	fur (on clothes)
frais (fraîche)	fresh
la fraise	strawberry
la framboise	raspberry
frapper	to hit
le frère	brother
le frigo	refrigerator
froid	cold (not hot)
le fromage	cheese
le fruit	fruit
la fusée	rocket
gagner	to win
le galet	pebble
le gant	glove
le garçon	boy
garder	to keep
la gare	station
garer	to park
le gâteau	cake
gauche	left
le gaz	gas
le géant	giant
geler	to freeze
génial	great, fantastic
le genou	knee
le genre	sort, type
les gens (m or f)	people
gentil (gentille)	kind, nice
la gerbille	gerbil
la girafe	giraffe
la glace	ice, ice cream
le glaçon	ice cube
glisser	to slide, to slip
se glisser	to creep

French word list

goûter	to taste	s'inscrire	to join (become a member)	leur, leurs	their
la goutte	drop			se lever	to stand up
grand	big, large, great, tall	l'insecte (m)	insect	la lèvre	lip
la grande personne	grown-up	l'instituteur (m)	teacher (m)	libre	free (not restricted)
		l'institutrice (f)	teacher (f)	le lieu	place
la grande ville	city	Internet (m)	Internet, the Net	la limace	slug
la grand-mère	grandmother	l'invitation (f)	invitation	le lion	lion
le grand-père	grandfather	l'invité (m)	guest, visitor (m)	lire	to read
les grands-parents (m)	grandparents	l'invitée (f)	guest, visitor (f)	lisse	smooth
		inviter	to invite	la liste	list
la grange	barn			le lit	bed
gratuit	free (no cost)	jamais	never	le livre	book
la grenouille	frog	la jambe	leg	loger	to stay (with someone)
grimper	to climb	janvier	January		
gris	gray	le jardin	garden	loin	far
gros (grosse)	big, large, great, fat	jaune	yellow	long (longue)	long
la grotte	cave	je	I	la longueur	length
le groupe	group	le jean	jeans	lourd	heavy
la guitare	guitar	jeter	to throw	lui	him, to or for him, to or for her
		le jeu	game		
s'habiller	to dress	jeudi	Thursday	la lumière	light
habiter	to live (in a place)	jeune	young	lundi	Monday
le hamburger	burger, hamburger	joli	pretty	la lune	moon
le hamster	hamster	jongler	to juggle	les lunettes (f)	glasses
le haricot	bean	jouer	to play	les lunettes de soleil (f)	sunglasses
haut	high	le jouet	toy		
le haut	top	le jour	day		
l'hélicoptère (m)	helicopter	le journal	newspaper	ma	my
l'herbe (f)	grass	la journée	day	la machine	machine
l'heure (f)	hour, time (on clock)	juillet	July	la machine à laver	washing machine
heure, heures	o'clock	juin	June		
heureux (heureuse)	happy	le jumeau	twin (m)	la magie	magic
		la jumelle	twin (f)	mai	May
heurter	to bump, to knock	la jungle	jungle	maigre	thin (person or animal)
le hibou	owl	la jupe	skirt		
hier	yesterday	le jus	juice	le maillot de bain	swimsuit
l'hippopotame (m)	hippopotamus, hippo	jusqu'à	until		
				la main	hand
l'histoire (f)	story	le kangourou	kangaroo	maintenant	now
l'hiver (m)	Winter			mais	but
hocher la tête	to nod	la	the, her	la maison	house, home
l'homme (m)	man	là	there	malheureux (malheureuse)	unhappy
l'hôpital (m)	hospital	le lac	lake		
l'horloge (f)	clock	laid	ugly	Maman	Mom
hors de	outside, out of	laisser	to leave (something), to let	Mamie	Grandma
le hot-dog	hotdog			le manche	handle (knife, pan)
l'hôtel (m)	hotel	laisser tomber	to drop	la manche	sleeve
l'huile (f)	oil	le lait	milk	le manchot	penguin
huit	eight	la laitue	lettuce	manger	to eat
huitième	eighth	la lampe	lamp	manquer	to be missing
hurler	to shout	le langage	language	le manteau	coat
		la langue	tongue, (foreign) language	le marché	market
ici	here			marcher	to walk, to work (machine)
l'idée (f)	idea	le lapin	rabbit		
il	he, it	large	wide	marcher à quatre pattes	to crawl
il y a	there's, there are	le lavabo	(bathroom) sink		
l'île (f)	island	laver	to wash	mardi	Tuesday
ils	they	se laver	to wash (yourself)	la marionnette	puppet
l'immeuble (m)	building	le	the, him	marron	brown
immobile	still, not moving	lécher	to lick	mars	March
impair	odd (number)	la leçon	lesson	le marteau	hammer
l'incendie (m)	house on fire	léger (légère)	light (not heavy)	le match	match (game)
indiquer	to point	le légume	vegetable	le matelot	sailor
l'infirmier (m)	nurse (m)	lent	slow	le matin	morning
l'infirmière (f)	nurse (f)	lentement	slowly	mauvais	bad, wrong
l'inondation (f)	flood	la lettre	letter	me	me

méchant	bad, wicked	le nœud	knot	Papi	Grandpa
le médecin	doctor	noir	black, dark	le papier	paper
le médicament	medicine	la noisette	hazelnut	le papillon	butterfly
le meilleur *or* la meilleure	best	la noix	nut, walnut	le papillon de nuit	moth
mélanger	to mix	le nom	name	par	through, done by
même	same	le nombre	number (quantity)	le parachute	parachute
mener	to lead	non	no	le parapluie	umbrella
mentir	to lie (not tell truth)	nos	our	le parc	park
		la note	note (music)	parce que	because
le menton	chin	notre	our	le parent	parent
la mer	sea	nouer	to tie	paresseux (paresseuse)	lazy
mercredi	Wednesday	le nounours	teddy bear		
la mère	mother	nous	we, us	parfois	sometimes
mes	my	nouveau (nouvel, nouvelle)	new	parler	to talk, to speak
le message	message			la part	slice, portion
mesurer	to measure	les nouvelles (f)	news	partager	to share
le métal	metal	novembre	November	la partie	part (of whole), game
mettre	to put	nu	bare	partir	to leave (a place)
le micro-ondes	microwave	le nuage	cloud	partout	everywhere
le miel	honey	la nuit	night	le passé	past
mignon (mignonne)	sweet, cute	nulle part	nowhere	passer	to pass (give)
		le numéro	number (street, phone)	se passer	to happen
le milieu	middle			passer devant	to pass (go past)
mille	thousand			la patte	paw
minuscule	tiny	occupé	busy	payer	to pay
la minute	minute	l'océan (m)	ocean	le pays	country, nation
le miroir	mirror	octobre	October	la peau	skin
le modèle	model	l'œil (m)	eye	la pêche	peach
le modèle réduit	(scale) model	l'œuf (m)	egg	pêcher	to fish
moi	me	l'oie (f)	goose	le peigne	comb
moi-même	myself	l'oignon (m)	onion	peindre	to paint
moins	less	l'oiseau (m)	bird	la peinture	paint
le mois	month	l'ombre (f)	shadow	la pelleteuse	digger
la moitié	half (portion)	l'oncle (m)	uncle	pencher	to lean
mon	my	l'ongle (m)	(finger)nail	pendant que	while
le monde	world	onze	eleven	pendre	to hang
la montagne	mountain	l'or (m)	gold	la pendule	clock
monter à cheval	to ride a horse	orange	orange (color)	penser	to think, to consider
la montgolfière	hot-air balloon	l'orange (f)	orange (fruit)	percuter	to crash
la montre	watch	l'orchestre (m)	band, orchestra	perdre	to lose
montrer	to show	l'ordinateur (m)	computer	le père	father
la moquette	carpet	l'oreille (f)	ear	le perroquet	parrot
mordre	to bite	l'oreiller (m)	pillow	personne	nobody, no one
le mot	word, note, message	organiser	to plan	la personne	person
la moto	motorcycle	l'orque (m)	killer whale	petit	small
la mouche	fly	l'orteil (m)	toe	le petit déjeuner	breakfast
mouillé	wet	l'os (m)	bone	le petit enfant	toddler
mourir	to die	ou	or	le petit pois	pea
le mouton	sheep	où	where	les petits-enfants (m)	grandchildren
le mur	wall	oublier	to forget		
mûr	ripe	oui	yes	peu	few
la musique	music	l'ours (m)	bear	peu profond	shallow
		ouvert	open	le phoque	seal
nager	to swim	ouvrir	to open	la photo	photo
la nature	nature	l'ovale (m)	oval	la phrase	sentence
le navire	ship			le piano	piano
la neige	snow	la page	page	la pièce	piece, part, coin, room (in house)
neiger	to snow	le pain	bread		
nettoyer	to clean	pair	even		
neuf	nine	la paire	pair	le pied	foot, base
neuf (neuve)	(brand) new	le palais	palace	la pierre	stone
neuvième	ninth	la palissade	fence	la pieuvre	octopus
le nez	nose	le pamplemousse	grapefruit	le pilote	pilot
le nid	nest	le panier	basket	le pique-nique	picnic
Noël	Christmas	le panneau	(road) sign	piquer	to sting
		Papa	Dad	le pire *or* la pire	worst

French word list

la piscine	swimming pool
la pizza	pizza
la place	room, space, seat (place to sit)
la plage	beach
le plan	plan
la planète	planet
la plante	plant
plat	flat
plein	full
pleurer	to cry
pleuvoir	to rain
plier	to fold
plonger	to dive
le plongeur	diver
la pluie	rain
plus	more
le plus *or* la plus	most
la poche	pocket
le poème	poem
les poils (m)	fur
le point	point (score)
la pointe	point (sharp)
pointu	sharp, pointed
la poire	pear
le poisson	fish
le poivre	pepper (spice)
le poivron	pepper (vegetable)
la police	police
la pomme	apple
la pomme de terre	potato
le pompier	firefighter
le pont	bridge
la porte	door
porter	to carry, to wear
poser	to put (down)
le pot	jar
le pouce	thumb
le poulain	foal
la poule	hen
le poulet	chicken
la poupée	doll
pour	for
pourquoi	why
poursuivre	to chase
pousser	to grow, to push
le poussin	chick
se précipiter	to rush
premier (première)	first
prendre	to take
près	close
presque	almost
prêt	ready
le prince	prince
la princesse	princess
principal	main
le printemps	Spring
le prix	price, prize
prochain	next, following
le professeur	teacher
profond	deep
promettre	to promise
propre (after noun)	clean
propre (before noun)	own
la prune	plum
puis	then
le puzzle	jigsaw puzzle
quand	when
la quantité	amount
quarante	forty
le quart	quarter
quatorze	fourteen
quatre	four
quatre-vingts	eighty
quatre-vingt-dix	ninety
quatrième	fourth
que	than, that, which, what (in questions)
quel, quelle, quels, quelles	which (in questions)
quelqu'un, quelqu'une	somebody, someone, anybody, anyone
quelque chose	something, anything
quelque part	somewhere, anywhere
la question	question
la queue	tail
qui	who
quinze	fifteen
raccommoder	to mend
raconter	to tell (story)
la radio	radio
la radiographie	x-ray (photo)
raide	steep, straight (hair)
le raisin	grape
le raisin sec	raisin
la rangée	line (of people)
se rappeler	to remember
le rat	rat
rater	to miss (not catch or hit)
le rayon x	x-ray
le rectangle	rectangle
le réfrigérateur	refrigerator
regarder	to look, to watch
la règle	ruler
la reine	queen
remarquer	to notice
remercier	to thank
remplir	to fill
remuer	to stir
le renard	fox
rencontrer	to meet (by chance)
renverser	to knock over, to spill
réparer	to mend, to fix
le repas	meal
repérer	to spot
répondre	to reply
la réponse	answer
le requin	shark
respirer	to breathe
rester	to stay
rétrécir	to shrink
retrouver	to meet (by arrangement)
réussir	to pass (a test)
le rêve	dream
réveiller	to wake
se réveiller	to wake up
le rhinocéros	rhinoceros, rhino
le rhume	cold (illness)
riche	rich
rien	nothing
rire	to laugh
la rivière	river
le riz	rice
la robe	dress
le robot	robot
robuste	strong, sturdy
le rocher	rock
le rock	rock (music)
le roi	king
rond	round
la rose	rose
rose	pink
la roue	wheel
rouge	red
la route	road
le ruban	ribbon
la rue	street
sa	his, her, its
le sable	sand
le sac	bag
sage	good (child)
la saison	season
la salade	salad, lettuce
sale	dirty
la salle de classe	classroom
saluer	to wave
salut	hello (to friends)
samedi	Saturday
la sandale	sandal
le sandwich	sandwich
sans intérêt	dull, boring
la saucisse	sausage
le saucisson	salami
sauf (sauve)	safe (and sound)
sauf si	unless
sauter	to jump
sauter à cloche-pied	to hop
sauvage	wild
sauver	to rescue, to save
savoir	to know (facts)
le savon	soap
le scarabée	beetle
la scie	saw
le scooter	(motor) scooter
le seau	bucket
sec (sèche)	dry
sécher	to dry
secouer	to shake
le secret	secret
seize	sixteen
le sel	salt
la selle	saddle
la semaine	week
le sentier	path

sentir	to smell	le tableau	picture	tu	you
se sentir	to feel	le tabouret	stool	tuer	to kill
sept	seven	la tache	spot		
septembre	September	la taille	size, height	un *or* une	a, one
septième	seventh	le tambour	drum	une fois	once
le serpent	snake	la tante	aunt	utile	useful
la serrure	lock	le tapis	rug		
le serveur	waiter	tard	late (near the end)	la vache	cow
la serveuse	waitress	la tasse	cup	la vague	wave
la serviette	towel	le taxi	taxi	le vaisseau spatial	spacecraft
se servir	to use	la télé	TV	la valise	suitcase
ses	his, her, its	le téléphone	telephone, phone	le vase	vase
seul	alone	la télévision	television	le veau	calf
seulement	just, only	la tempête	storm	le vélo	bicycle
le shampooing	shampoo	le temps	time (taken), weather	vendre	to sell
le short	shorts			vendredi	Friday
si	if, so (so big), yes (contradicting)	tenir	to hold (in your hands)	venir	to come
s'il te plaît	please	la tente	tent	le vent	wind
s'il vous plaît	please	terne	dull (color)	le verre	glass
le siège	seat	la terre	earth, floor, land, soil	vert	green
signer	to sign			la veste	jacket
silencieux (silencieuse)	quiet, silent	tes	your	les vêtements (m)	clothes
		la tête	head	la viande	meat
le singe	ape, monkey	le thé	tea	vide	empty
six	six	le ticket	ticket (bus, subway)	la vie	life
sixième	sixth	le tigre	tiger	vieux (vieil, vieille)	old
la sœur	sister	le timbre	stamp	vif (vive)	bright
le soir	evening	tirer	to pull	vilain	naughty
soixante	sixty	le toast	toast	la ville	town
soixante-dix	seventy	le toboggan	slide	vingt	twenty
le sol	ground	la toile	web	violet (violette)	purple
le soldat	soldier	les toilettes (f)	restroom	le visage	face
le soleil	sun	le toit	roof	la visière	peak (cap)
le sommet	peak (mountain)	la tomate	tomato	visiter	to visit
son	his, her, its	tomber	to fall	vite	fast, quick
sonner	to ring, to sound	ton	your	vivre	to live, to be alive
la sorcière	witch	tôt	early	le vœu	wish
le sort	spell	toucher	to touch, to feel	voici	here's, this is
la sorte	sort	toujours	always	voir	to see
la soucoupe	saucer	tourner	to turn	le voisin	neighbor (m)
souffler	to blow	le tournesol	sunflower	la voisine	neighbor (f)
soulever	to lift	tous (toutes)	all	la voiture	car
la soupe	soup	tout (toute)	all, each, every	la voiture de police	police car
sourire	to smile	tout à coup	suddenly		
la souris	mouse	tout à fait	quite, completely	la voiture de pompiers	fire engine
sous	below, under	tout le monde	everybody, everyone		
se souvenir	to remember	le tracteur	tractor	la voix	voice
souvent	often	le train	train	voler	to fly, to steal
spécial	special	le trait	line (in drawing)	vos	your
le sport	sports	tranchant	sharp (cutting)	votre	your
la star	star (famous person)	la tranche	slice (of bread, meat)	vouloir	to want
le stylo	pen	tranquille	still, calm	vouloir dire	to mean
le sucre	sugar	travailler	to work (do a job)	vous	you
sucré	sweet (taste)	traverser	to cross	le voyage	journey
super	great, fantastic	treize	thirteen	vrai	real, true
le supermarché	supermarket	trente	thirty	la vue	view
sur	on (top of), about	très	very		
sûr	sure, safe (not dangerous)	le triangle	triangle	les WC (m)	toilet
		triste	sad	le Web	(World Wide) Web
la surprise	surprise	trois	three		
le symbole	sign, symbol	troisième	third	le xylophone	xylophone
sympa	friendly, nice	la trottinette	scooter		
		le trou	hole	le zèbre	zebra
ta	your	trouver	to find	zéro	zero
la table	table	le t-shirt	T-shirt	le zoo	zoo

Hear the words on the Internet

If you can use the Internet and your computer can play sounds, you can listen to all the French words and phrases in this dictionary, read by a French person.

Go to the Usborne Quicklinks Web site at **www.usborne-quicklinks.com** Type in the keywords **french picture dictionary** and follow the simple instructions. Try listening to the words or phrases and then saying them yourself. This will help you learn to speak French easily and well.

Always follow the safety rules on the right when you are using the Internet.

What you need

To play the French words, your computer may need a small program called an audio player, such as

RealPlayer® or Windows® Media Player. These programs are free, and if you don't already have one, you can download a copy from **www.usborne-quicklinks.com**

Internet safety rules

- Ask your parent's, guardian's or teacher's permission before you connect to the Internet.
- When you are on the Internet, never tell anyone your full name, address or telephone number, and ask an adult before you give your e-mail address.
- If a Web site asks you to log in or register by typing your name or e-mail address, ask an adult's permission first.
- If you receive an e-mail from someone you don't know, tell an adult and do not reply to the e-mail.

Notes for parents or guardians

The Picture Dictionary area of the Usborne Quicklinks Web site contains no links to external Web sites. However, other areas of Usborne Quicklinks do contain links to Web sites that do not belong to Usborne Publishing. The links are regularly reviewed and updated, but Usborne Publishing is not responsible, and does not accept liability, for the content or availability of any Web site other than its own, or for any exposure to harmful, offensive or inaccurate material which may appear on the Web.

We recommend that children are supervised while on the Internet, that they do not use Internet Chat Rooms and that you use Internet filtering software to block unsuitable material. Please ensure that your children follow the safety guidelines above. For more information, see the "Net Help" area on the Usborne Quicklinks Web site at **www.usborne-quicklinks.com**

RealPlayer® is a trademark of RealNetworks, Inc., registered in the US and other countries.
Windows® is a trademark of Microsoft Corporation, registered in the US and other countries.

With thanks to Staedtler for providing the Fimo® material for models.
Bruder® toys supplied by Euro Toys and Models Ltd.
Additional models by Les Pickstock, Barry Jones, Stef Lumley, Karen Krige and Stefan Barnett
Americanization editor: Carrie Seay

First published in 2002 by Usborne Publishing Ltd, 83-85 Saffron Hill, London EC1N 8RT, England. www.usborne.com
Copyright © 2002 Usborne Publishing Ltd. First published in America in 2003.

The name Usborne and the devices 🎈🎈 are Trade Marks of Usborne Publishing Ltd. All rights reserved. No part of this publication may be reproduced, stored in a retrieval system, or transmitted by any means, electronic, mechanical, photocopying, recording or otherwise, without the prior permission of the publisher. AE. Printed in Italy.